Deleted Scenes from the Bestselling Utopian Novel

Vanya Bagaev

Nova Nevédoma

Nova Nevédoma

nova-nevedoma.com

Deleted Scenes from the Bestselling Utopian Novel
Vanya Bagaev © 2024

ISBN: PB: 978-1-0687677-0-8
HC: 978-1-0687677-2-2
eBook: 978-1-0687677-1-5

Contents

To: The illustrious Editor-in-Chief

Subject: Deliberation on Deleted Scenes from the
Bestselling Utopian Novel

Esteemed Editor-in-Chief,

As the Editorial Committee, we present this succi-
nt report including the excisioned sequence from the
bestselling utopian novel. Our actions were undertaken
to preserve narrative integrity and avoid the descent
into lierary anarchy and narrative discord.

Post-examination, our expert collective determined
that the deleted sequence suffered from turgid grandi--
loquence, non sequiturs and obfuscations, creating a
disjointed reading experience. We have concluded that
these sequences cannot be reinstated without comprimi-
sing the novel's status as an exemplar of utopian literature. As a committee, we have acted in the best interests of literary excellence and the written word.

Hereby we provide you with the deleted scenes and
humbly anticipate your concurrence with our verdict a-
nd await your guidance on any further course of action

In sincere obeisance,

Editorial Committee

I

№1.1: Lacuna

Every snowflake that settles on the frozen city carries the weight of silent dissent. Buried under the drifts, we gather our strength, stretch out our hands and soar. It is but a lurid dream, we know, for that is the only time when we can fly. Our wings draped in snow, we, a lonely androgynous angel, sweep over the age-bleached streets, peering into the windows of grey houses where corpses try to tune into Channel One. The screens show nothing but static that taunts them and, lost and distressed, the corpses smash their black boxes, bend the aerials, twist the knobs, yet nothing happens, nothing — the static does not disappear and they give up. They approach the window, and the first thing they see is an angel with wings blinding white. Oh, they envy us, they envy our graceful flight, frown, and grind their teeth, while we, angelically apathetic, dismiss their existence. Eyes closed, we whirl round the towering buildings as the corpses boil oil on their foil-covered rusty kitchen hobs, and the moment we pass by their windows, all together they douse us with the bubbling liquid. The oil sizzles and splashes, our white wings disintegrate, the skin on our face peels away to expose the bare flesh beneath, we scream and

A cacophony of thundering footsteps and demonic voices outside our flat on the landing jolts us awake. Sweating and cold, we crawl out of the bed and cocoon ourselves in a thick quilt. Clocks tick in the kitchen, floorboards creak; a draught slithers across the floor. After us? Silent, alone, we float through our flat doorwards. The quilt keeps our pale body warm, fighting the surrounding chill that controls everything: the air, the floor, the blood, and the cold metal door against our cheek.

You're the one who forgot to close the window yesterday.

Through the wide-angle lens of the spyhole, a crystal ball, we look into the landing, our dry eyes irritated by reality's luridness. There on the landing, faceless demons, clad in black ski suits and balaclavas, have gathered under a nervous bulb at a neighbour's door, and, hands crossed, stand stroking their big black batons.

They exchange professional trifles, cursing and sneering, expressing dissatisfaction over the late — nay, early — foray, while simmering in suspense. One of them, a rookie, trembles and paces back and forth, checking his watch, which draws mockery of his unprofessional nerves. The most rotund of the demons shakes his head, shushes the crew, then presses the doorbell's button deep into the white wall.

Bzzzzzzzz!

Another starts pounding the metal door with his clumsy fist, again and again. The industrial din reverberates through the landing while another demon with a chief's demeanour beholds the scene, leaning against the wall, puffing clouds of acrid smoke.

Thirty-eight seconds later, the lock rattles, and the door hesitantly opens to reveal a young man, crumpled, shaggy, and still lethargic, as if his body alone has come out to greet the visitors, his mind lingering in dreams, like our own, like this one, a beginning of a nightmare. Upon seeing the uninvited guests, his empty sleepy eyes brim with vivacity. The narcotic scent of adrenaline invades the landing and wafts under every door.

Without warning, the bellringer violently grabs the man and drags him out of the flat and onto the landing. In one fluid motion, he forces both of the man's arms behind him and shoves his face against the white wall. The man groans, struggling to break free. Meanwhile, two of the crew enter the flat and dissolve into the darkness.

Gnashing his teeth to dust, the man retorts:

—The fuck?!

The bellringer, baton in hand, responds with a vicious blow to the man's ribs, forcing a guttural cry and the breath from his lungs to echo throughout the landing. More savage blows follow.

—Shut your fucking gob, you twat!

—What did I do?

—What? Forgot them fucking "peace" posters you scrawled, didn't you?

—What posters? I didn't scrawl a bloody thing.

—"I didn't scrawl a bloody thing", he says. Some sort of "Abstractionist," aren't you?

—I don't know what the fuck you're on about!

—He's against his country, lads.

Together they start enacting a grotesque pantomime. It's difficult to assign the words to any of the figures on the landing — demons and our neighbour included — as the whole scene appears as a singular speaking object.

—Tell us, don't you love your motherland, you fucking prick?

—Or the Tsar? Huh?

—He reckons we lay down arms and surrender, so he does.

—Well then, I'd reckon he's a traitor, wouldn't you lot?

—I'd reckon he is. A fucking traitor.

—I haven't done anything! I haven't said a goddamn word!

The man desperately struggles to break free from the bellringer's inexorable grip.

—What sort of women even spawn such worthless blighters!

—Whores.

—Filthy fucking whores, aye.

—Always the whores. Uh-huh.

—You've got the wrong man! I'll call the police!

—Go ahead, squeal, snitch — We don't give a fuck, we **are** the police.

The bellringer hurls the man to the floor and continues beating him. Each hit makes him convulse and yell, but his cries aren't loud enough, so the demon decides to use his legs to reach the desired volume of pain.

—I didn't do anything! Bastards! You're all bastards!

—Lost your nerve, have you, huh?

Another demon joins the operation, booting the man in the kidney area, until he falls silent and curls in on himself. Each thud echoes through the hall so even our door vibrates.

—Assaulting a police officer!

Thud.

—Resisting arrest!

Thud.

—Defaming the army!

Thud.

—His motherland fucking spoon-feeds him, and he slings it through the muck.

—Bloody wanker.

—Cocksucker.

—Fucking crybaby, all you lot want to do is whinge, make your fucking snow angels, scrawl your fucking rubbish, never doing a real fucking job.

—I didn't...

—Yelling in the streets during the day, at home during the night, disturbing neighbours.

—Anti-social behaviour, that.

—Ahhh!

—Yeah, there you have it.

—Nothing but a crybaby.

—Go on, call your mum, you fucker. I said call your fucking whore!

The spyhole fogs up, blurring our view of the unfolding operation. With a jittery hand, we wipe away the condensation with a corner of our quilt. In suffocating, tomb-like stillness, our finger lingers around the cover of the spyhole, ensuring it doesn't close.

The man wraps himself in his own arms, shielding his stomach and face with his legs.

—Bloody immortal, are you? No respect for the police!

The man's resistance only seems to rouse the demons further, fuelling their sadistic enthusiasm for the operation. As a cat plays with a mouse, observes it, waits for it to move, touches it gently with its paw, the demons wait for something to ignite their inflamed centres of violence, at least a little trigger, a click that would tell them they can lift the batons into the air again and continue the game. The chief, meanwhile, is satisfied. He languishes, watching as if the whole event has been performed just for him.

Trembling, his face bruised, the man huddles in a corner, moaning and sniffling, and tries to fuse through the wall, but the bellringer snatches and hauls him to the staircase rail, sharply wrests his left arm upwards until something crunches, and the man shrieks.

—So, "angel"? Answer me, can you fucking fly?

—I didn't do a thing...—the man mumbles, sobbing.

—Quit your gabbing! Answer me!

The demon bends the man's upper torso over the rail and smashes his spine with the baton, causing him to lose balance, but he immediately grabs hold of the rail, coughs, and spits blood.

We wonder, isn't it astonishing how our neighbour, whose name we don't know despite surely having brushed past him in the lift a few times, is so resilient and still alive? We would have passed out long ago, or would have taken the opportunity right at that moment to hurl our body down the shaft to relieve it of the demons.

Yes, no doubt, you'd do exactly that!

The third door on the landing creaks and a sleepy, grey-haired lady in a long nightdress materialises, more baffled than terrified. Upon seeing her, the demons freeze like mannequins and only continue to pant and wheeze under their balaclavas like pigs after a marathon. Our neighbour, still bent over the rail, looks mournfully at the old lady. A thin, red line of blood and saliva seeps from his split lip.

—What on earth are you doing, boys...—whispers the old lady, covering her mouth with both hands.

As she recoils, one of them steps towards her and raises his fist menacingly.

—At your age... you'd better mind your own business, ma'am,—he hisses, slamming the door shut in front of her face, and leans on it, his hulking frame obscuring the spyhole.

The bellringer drags the man off the rail and forces him face down on the floor. Looming over him, he growls:

—Look...

The man lies motionless, holding his breath, his face pressed against the floor.

—Look, I said!—shouts the bellringer. He grabs the man's head and flashes the baton, waving it.—I'm gonna flay your arse into bloody ribbons with this fucking thing and then baptise you in piss, get it?

He snarls and starts pushing the baton between the man's buttocks through his trousers.

At that moment, his two comrades exit the man's flat, their hands bereft of bounty, their heads shaking in disappointment.

—Nothing! Not a single fucking thing! We fucking turned the fucking dump upside down and found fucking nothing,—squeaks one, stuttering curses.

—No illegal posters, guv, no brushes or pencils. No "prohibited literature". Not even drugs. Bloody nothing.

—You know why, you fuckwits?

They stare at the chief, bewildered.

—Because I said "fifteen" and not fucking "fifty", you stupid cunts. I wondered if you would fucking deduce that! Get the fuck out of here!

—But guv...

—Leave the lad alone, I said!

That twist plunges the bellringer into a state of primal fury. He starts shaking, clenches his fists and growls like a rabid hyena whose meal has been snatched away. If we were a dog or a wolf, we would have heard the pounding pulse of the demon's heart, felt how his entire body reeked with rage radiating from every crevice, encasing him in a shimmering crimson aura.

One of the demons checks the spyhole of the old lady's flat but sees nothing, because, to his misfortune, that's not how spyholes work. He tries summoning the lift, but it remains stubbornly non-functional. Frustrated, he jabs at the button, yet nothing happens again.

—Fucking tin can!

The bellringer strikes our quivering neighbour with his baton one more time, spits on his back, then follows the others to the stairs. The chief, on his way there, bends over the man's swollen face, clicks his tongue multiple times, shakes his head, and says:

—And you, stay put, lie low and rest. It ain't no good insulting police officers. Remember.

An icy chill creeps up our spine. We exhale, choke down the invisible rock scraping against our parched throat, and quickly seal the spyhole.

№1.2: Schism

There's that strange feeling that a new, hitherto unknown stratum of reality has peeled off like a scabbed blister from the main life strata, where all, both good and evil, is, for better or worse, sorted out, simple, comprehensible, and ignorable.

Ignorable on demand.

Our neighbour will manage, or the old lady will help him, for she, with her kind, caring, and motherly heart, would do a better job of it than us. We aren't being apathetic, are we?

Oh, of course, you're not.

The demons might come for us, too.

You've done nothing wrong, or nothing right, or nothing at all.

If we do nothing and keep our mouths and doors shut, nobody will find us lurking in our flat 53, will they? It's us alone: flesh and phantasm, atom and abstraction, microcosm and macrocosm—a universe unto ourselves. We can ignore everything else, can't we?

You can't see anything with your metaphorical cataracts. Your blindness is your bliss.

And the phone, the phone too, we mustn't pick up a handset.

Don't leave your room.

We should sleep, all day, all night. We need a coma.

You can't sleep within a dream, can you? Even if now it's a part of

Nothing. Nothing is happening; minutes pass, hours, days, nobody comes, nobody knocks, nobody calls. It's just a ghost of us in an empty, cold flat alone with our thoughts, haunted by them. The vision of the outside world has gone nil. The sun is a parody of intermission in the unremitting winter nights. It is, in fact, not a star but a mere gas lantern with a lamplighter who is neither a night owl nor a morning lark, but a drunkard. A dense and damp fog, palpable if you open the window and try to feel it with your fingers, veils everything beyond a few metres, and the world becomes white, as if we, on our thirteenth floor, live in a concrete box somewhere in cloudy cuckoo land, and all we have left to do is to gaze into the white wall and let our brain do a photomontage of images, a kaleidoscope, a labyrinth of what-ifs, with or without permission from our free will. Books are impotent word-coffins—the number of our thoughts flashing simultaneously eclipses anything that the author could condense into her creation, failing to compete with our mind. Thank you, author, we have enough of our own thoughts to think. We like thinking thoughts. They are perfectly thinkable. In fact, each of our thoughts is an author itself, an autonomous agent that keeps seething inside our mind, writing stories, so all we have left to do is to surrender, succumb, stare into the emptiness on the other side of the window and let each story unfold. Oh, they end terribly; the best thing that can happen in them is nothing, and the best we can hope for is no resolution. Otherwise, there's always somebody beaten or dead, or not some- but everybody. It's much better when the story frac- tures, breaks off and diverges, as if the author is knackered from writing it and switches to a new one, more interesting, where, however, more interesting means more dismal, spawning numerous branches of inhumanity, which, no matter how we try to stifle them, evade and resurge in strange and unexpected places, like blackberry bushes taking over our granny's garden every summer anew. Not sure we want to tell any of these stories. Not sure we want to tell any story at all. It's better to tell something absurd, create a literary cage, the content of which cannot exist under any possible conditions anywhere and nowhere. Some stories must not see reality, for they may emerge into it, merge with it and make it far worse than it already is.

No, you can't make it worse than—

Death to the pigs.

Oh, this is surely an audacious one.

A lurid dream there was of a country where all law and military enforcement agencies metamorphosed into pig-faced, hoofed demons. Their tusks and horns grew as their anger and violence surged to the point where they could no longer stand on their hind legs like human beings and had to stand on all fours to move at all. Then, when the sharp offshoots could no longer extend due to the physical constraints of the subsequent enlargement, their bodies themselves began to swell, while the brain shrank, redirecting all the energy necessary into further demonification.

Oh, dear.

The apotheosis of their transformation was a cloven-hoofed behemoth two to three metres long, one and a half metres high, a couple of tonnes in weight, with huge black horns akin to mammoth tusks, but jagged in texture. The skin of such a creature would eventually turn red as if it had been stripped off altogether, revealing bare flesh. The creature would walk slowly, heavily, crumpling the floor beneath it, panting, snorting, and emitting a plume of pollution like an exhausted car muffler with a dirty or clogged air filter. This breed, *Homo Demonicus*, was cultivated by a professor in a laboratory, who, for some reason, looked like our late father. He had the same moustache, tobacco-stained and yellowed, an almost bald head, and ponderous, tortoise-rimmed spectacles that resembled two loupes. He wore a beige, once white, lab coat and carried a bulky, black ledger with pages falling out of it in random places. This was at least how we remember him, when he worked at the university, with the only exception—he didn't wear a lab coat then, because why would a historian work in a lab and need a lab coat?

One has to be well-versed in history to produce a breed of absolute cruelty.

The laboratory was located deep in the undercity, in one of the abandoned metro lines, and looked like an endless prison corridor, a gallery of the damned, flanked by hollowed cells with bars behind which shackled bodies dwelled. Every morning, the professor made his rounds, driving through the eerie expanse in a crumbling, creaking draisine controlled by service personnel, a medium-sized demon with an overcooked broccoli for a brain. The draisine would stop at each cell, and the professor would pant as he hopped off, open the lattice with a key, and take a bottle-looking syringe of thick and muddy red sludge from the pocket of his beige lab coat to inject it into the subject, intravenously, summoning a fugue of tormented tones in D# minor. After a few such visits, the subject's skin turned red, its pupils narrowed goatly, its nasal structure morphed into a grotesque pig snout. Soft horns and fangs began to grow, and so on exponentially until

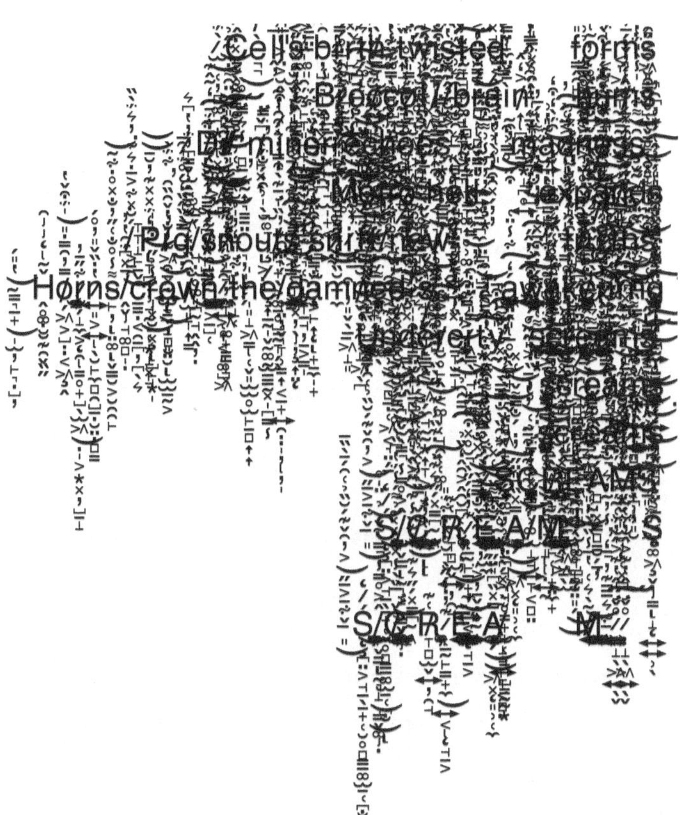
Cells birth twisted forms
Broccoli brain
Of mind
Metamorph expands
Pig/snout sniff new
Horns/crown the damned awakening
S/CREAM
S/CREAM
S/CREAM

Odd. They've started chatting to each other.

They who?

The thoughts, teeming.

Whose thoughts?

Ours. Can't you hear? They're oozing from the cracks of our collective consciousness.

Oh, are they? Lovely.

Yes, and they are exchanging opinions.

This is nonsense. Stop it. Who cares about your thoughts?

They themselves seem to care about themselves and that's enough.

Uh-huh.

From ætherial matter, silhouettes of thoughts mould. Their distant voices become louder and clearer. They, in unknown quantity and quality, all blurry—nay faceless—sit around the long table, no end of it seen. One after another, thoughts slam shots of strong spirits and engage in a civilised discourse:

—One wonders how much humanity remains in those demons after the metamorphosis. What is humanity anyway? He-he.

—That's a loaded term.

—It is indeed!

—Loaded with what?

—With cannonballs!

—With blueberries!

—With meanings!

—With nonsense!

—"The zenith of civilisation" *(the thought makes air quotes)*. On the journey to which we've discovered the concepts of sadism, genocide, slavery, countless types of torture and murder using a diverse list of tools and devices, as if a stone or a stick weren't enough for that!

—You forgot the batons. Big black ones.

—Hands will do!

—Nothing's better than a mindflay psyop, gentlemen. Ahem... and ladies.

—What about kindness, cooperation, creativity, culture, literature, technology, art, and science?

—As if it all holds any weight at this juncture.

—Kindness to the killers, cooperation with the demons, creativity in developing torture devices, culture of obedience, banned literature, military technology, art of war, and science of wilful ignorance.

—As much as flowers breaking through the cement. "In the midst of maelstrom, beauty blossoms," as one wise fellow said.

—Or rather destroyed. He-he.

—Who said that?

Sepulchral silence. The first thought refills the

shots and, following an unknowingly elongated intermission, continues:

—One wonders if they have a plan for beatings and torture, if they need to curry favour to receive more stars on shoulder straps, a flat, a car, a pension at thirty-five, or if it is all, as they say, personal initiative, the call of nature, adrenaline rush, an urge to prove to the world that they are worth something as they seek revenge on the world for their earlier treatment, for their childhood bullying, for someone stealing their first love. Or perhaps it's fear, the banal fear of losing the job you've dreamed of since a young age, telling your grandma that when you grow up, you'd become a policeman and protect her from bandits, a fear that later morphed into a dread of going to prison for not complying with the orders of those same bandits, or different ones, because you know that people like yourself will be watching you, and you know what they are.

—Perhaps they just believe in what they do and deem it "good", you know. If they aren't psychopaths, they must think they are doing a good thing, good job, all that, for a greater good.

—Blind pigs! Blind followers of the Tsar! He-he.

—It's all... *(the speaker hiccups)* because of "the red sludge". Oo-oo...

—Maybe soon, imminently, their helmets will

have holes to fit their gnarled goat's horns, still little and soft, only yet to jut. Soon, very soon, their pupils will become goatly, cowardly vertical.

—Could it be the reason why they wear balaclavas and helmets? To hide who they are?

—Maybe there are no faces there anymore. Maybe they aren't human beings at all, but swinish demons ashamed to look people in the eye.

Is it a dark fantasy novel or what?

—The greatest tragedy is that no matter what we say here, no matter how much we try to squeeze out a metaphor or a nice word, neither that metaphor nor that word will ever be heard by the person they are denouncing; not because they can't read—they very much can—but because they don't care about our indignation, our pain and discontent. They don't care about humanity, morality, ethics, faith, hope, or love.

—They do care about love. At least subconsciously, they crave it even more than power.

—They have morals but for us they are "immoral". He-he. Same with the faith and all those fancy things.

—Oh, well...

—Their sole desire is to turn us all into blood-thirsty demons with "Thou shalt kill" engraved on our subcortex!

—In capital letters. Without punctuation!

—How on Earth would you punctuate that?

—Why would "angels" want more demons in the world?

—Should we descend to their level, spew blood on everything our species has achieved and revert to barbarism, all the while desiring that barbarism to end? One wise fellow said that one cannot teach pity, intelligence, logic and awareness for decades and centuries with impunity.

—Who said that?

—It is possible to get used to the sight of blood, tears, suffering, and death—like butchers or doctors; but how is it possible, having reached the truth after epochs of killing and destruction, to simply relinquish it? It is absurd!

—As another wise fellow said, "It's not absurd! It's far worse—it's a tradition!"

The thoughts laugh and clink shots.

—What for?

—Who the fuck said that?

—"What for" what?

—What do you propose? Sit back on a sofa, chill, and watch them beat, torture, and imprison our friends and neighbours?

—I propose we do everything within and beyond our power, but still remain human in all this!

—How's that?

—Tongue and ears! We can talk and listen! Can

you hear it? I'm TALKING. We can communicate our ideas, engage in dialogue; argue, damn it! Not just with them—at least start with each other!

—Well, we're doing that now. Where is this all going, eh?

—Why beat and shiv the undesirable? Strangle, torture, stab, drown, rape with batons? Is that what you call *Homo sapiens*?

—I'm not saying anything. It's your rant. But it seems to me that we failed to devise more efficient methods of communication.

—But how...

—Demons can only be defeated by other demons; all the angels could do was segregate the demons and let them breed, for whatever reason.

—I'm confused.

—I know the reason, but I won't tell you lot! Too dark!

—It's obvious: so they themselves could live their naive, angelic lives, all white and innocent. As one wise fellow said, "If you want to get through a door, knock".

—Who? Please...

—*The angels locked themselves in hell, la la-la la-la. Oi!*

—I'm not going to knock. Haven't you understood? Haven't I made it clear?

—The thing is, if you don't knock them down first, they will knock down you. You should be one step ahead and knock "preventively".

—Knock-knock. Who's there?

—Those are their methods. You're using their own linguistic legerdemain. This is what we're fighting against, isn't it?!

—Oh, are we fighting something? Sometimes I forget.

—It's so easy to forget, ladies and gentlemen.

—Such a subtle guerrilla fight! He-he.

—We have three choices: fight, flee, or hang yourself. In the end, the only ones left are those who can fight and sell ropes.

—And soap! And soa... oops.

—That's what I'm talking about—we're going backwards! Into the barbaric abyss!

—There's no binary direction, it is helical, mind you.

—Alright, quiet please. A thought experiment: let's say a man corners you, his fists flailing. What would you do?

—What if the man has a knife?

—Kick the bucket!

—You can negotiate, you can offer him some terms. Why would he want blood on his hands? Is that what he wants, rather than, say, going home to his family, having a drink, watching the telly together?

—Did you ask him?

—About what?

—Does the blood on his hands bother him, and does he want to have a chat with you about his *modus vivendi*? During the day, he goes to work, presses buttons, fires missiles at peaceful cities, and in the evening, he goes home, kisses his child on the forehead, they all have dinner together and go to bed. And he takes out a knife because he's utterly fed up with you, inordinately irritated, or fucking annoyed, in simple terms, and not because he questions your ethics. You run around shouting about how terrible he is, how he is a disgusting, cruel animal that treats you so badly and doesn't let you breathe, while he sits there, reddening, riling, sharpening his knife...

—We should have started talking to each other earlier!

—We should have started killing each other earlier!

—It's never too late, dear friends. Such a noble pursuit!

—... And he doesn't want to listen to you; he doesn't, and he never has. Why should he care about you? Who are you to him? He's your leader, your leech, your lord, and your liege—all those things. He does everything for you (so he thinks), and you still want something, some kind of freedoms, rights, that humanist bullshit...

—We aren't humanists here!

—To continue with our first question, what is humanity anyway?

—... He does not think in these categories; they are nonsense for him, a sheer absurdity in the same way as you are an ungrateful wretch who shows no respect and wishes only harm, yells, and whines, using, by the way, quite invective words. He's scared of you, and then, when the fear has nowhere to go, he becomes infuriated.

—Well, we should teach him!

—We should have taught him earlier!

—"Fear to Fury Dynamics 101".

—We should have... punched him in the face, for one, before he sharpened his knife; that's what we should've done. And now... here we are. It's a zero-sum game. Admit it and make a choice.

—I will not wield a weapon; I won't kill!

—I don't want to kill either. But with weapons, it's more persuasive.

—I saw bullfinches the other day, cute little apples.

—As one wise fellow said, "The vileness of the methods translates into the vileness of the results."

—Let me translate it for you.

—Who?!

—Even if we kill all the killers, only killers will remain!

—Huh! So, let's hear your plan, eh? Pray tell.

—A million people on the streets, a million shouting, "We can't take this anymore!", a million showing by example what peace is like—that's what's impressive, that's what's loud.

—The truth is that all who have gathered from that million are us, thoughts of just one person.

—And imagine how many thoughts like us are out there!

—Many, perhaps, but the thing is, we remain in people's hea—

At that moment, the door to the room where thoughts have been residing blasts off its hinges and falls into the corridor. It is knocked out with a single, but well-practised *knock-knock*. The thoughts shudder, one of them drops a bottle; it shatters, the pieces of glass scatter around, and the strong spirit spills out onto the floor. A squad of armoured demons charges into the room, bellowing out commands in Demonesque and waving their guns around.

—To the floor! Everybody on the floor!

—I said, get down!

—Hands behind your back!

One of the demons fires a warning shot, and heavy snowflakes of plaster fall down and cover the cowering thoughts.

—You fucking move, and the next one goes through your skull!

The thoughts are paralysed, mortified. They have been hunted down, cornered, suppressed.

—Lie down! Don't move!

The cow says "moo", the goat says "maa", the horse says "neigh", and the pig says:

—You have the right to remain silent. You are being charged with propaganda for pacifism!

Thus lie our thoughts, kissing the floor, unable to be thought no more.

One doesn't want to impute insanity to the demons; it's certain they are in control, at least now, even if they are only following orders. A swollen sense of self-importance has metastasised throughout their bodies, and a cascade of maladies has appeared: inflammation of impunity; collapse of the moral compass; chronic itching of the anger organ; uncontrollable violent disorder; atrophy of kindness; acute lack of empathy; weakened immunity to inhumane orders; critical thinking deficit syndrome; hypertrophy of the ego; tunnel vision of righteousness; paralysis of conscience; autoimmune rejection of mercy; sepsis of the soul. Of course, it must be an occupational deformity, something they acquire in the course of their work, losing sensitivity to violence, blood, and gore, like butchers or doctors. *Or historians.* But what if only ones like them get the job?

The white canvas morphs into a grey room with a flickering and crackling yellow fluorescent lamp hanging above a big stainless steel desk. There sit face-to-face two faceless thoughts: an interviewer with a woman's silhouette and an interviewee with a man's silhouette.

—Tell us about your strengths,—asks the woman.

The faceless man scratches his head.

—Well... that's erm...—he stammers.—I don't know how to put it.

—Whatever it is, just say it. That will determine whether or not we hire you for the job.

Silence. The man cracks his knuckles and then looks the faceless woman straight in the eyes.

—I can fuck someone's face up,—he whispers.

She licks her lips and whispers back:

—Just a face? Hm...

Crickets. The lamp crackles like lightning through the clear sky.

—Well, not only a face, of course.

—Something else, perhaps?

She leans closer to the interviewee.

—Well, anything, it doesn't matter. Whatever you ask.

—For example? We need you to be very precise. It's important for the evaluation of your professional capabilities.

—Erm...—he hesitates.—Kidneys, I can fuck someone's kidneys up.

—Huh... And that's it?—she says and leans back, disappointed.—Have you even tortured anyone?

A shadow flushes on the interviewee's face. He says nothing, his eyes on the table.

—Well... may... maybe.

Pause. The interviewer taps her nails on the metal table.

—Do you beat your wife?

—Well... I don't know how to put it.

She squirms in her chair.

—Just say it. As I said, we need to build a psychological profile of you, to assess your skills and understand if you're a good fit for the job.

—I do...—says the man and gulps loudly.—In my house, I have a basement. So... And... Sometimes, I... erm... torture cats there. Every Tuesday, in fact.

She gulps, and a lonely brow arches on her face.

—Oh... quite commendable. Why not on Mondays?

—It's kittens, to be precise,—says the man nervously.—Little squeaky ones. Black.

An orgasmic spasm goes through the interviewer's body, and her chair shrieks.

—Wondrous! Just wondrous! Exactly what we're looking for, young man. Congratulations, you're hired!

Two visions on the canvas never merge: one eye perceives, the other eye distorts, a diptych of reality and truth. They seem to be the same, yet superimposed, vertigo they birth, a nausea that persists behind closed lids, in dream realm where our moored head floats like a boat fixed in place. On the telly, in the newspapers, and on the radio, there's a utopia on the brink of bursting into the blindingly bright future, while outside the window, there's emptiness, darkness, vibrating void. Next door, torture's rhythms, screams of pain and crimson sludge, an aura; nearby, a snow angel earns a one-way passage to kátorga. Of war they whisper, peace they scream aloud till throats run raw. Dirt, slush, frost, bursting pipes and capillaries, blood on the staircase in the entrance hall; all walls are cracked, but through them, flowers seek the light. Utopian weed blooms in the mind's rifts, but withers, plagued, once skull is left behind. As it turns out, one needs not lay a stone to build utopia; one can convince the rest they live in one already.

In the smoky room, the highest echelons of

thought lounge on mahogany chairs at a round table, also mahogany, and share strong spirits, of an expensive kind, sipping them from gold-encrusted cat skulls.

—Well, listen, dear sir, does war have a place in utopias?

—It does not, of course.

—Then what are you trying to peddle to us? War in utopias? Sir, you ought to take some pills, clear your head,—the thought remarks, twisting at the temple.—He-he.

—Valid point! What are you trying to peddle to us? As the engineers of this whole mess, we pay the utmost attention to such details. He-he-he.

—Hold on a minute, dear sirs...—the thought interjects and clears its throat.—You're neglecting the most basic knowledge: in any utopia, if one digs deep enough, one is bound to find a candied piece of shite.

The room is abuzz.

—Oh, come on, so candid of you!—exclaims the thought and theatrically waves its hands.

The other thought attempts to calm the room down.

—Dear sirs, watch yourselves, please. Not at the table!

—"Excrements", if that's how you prefer it, dear sir. Doesn't change the essence of it, though, does it?

—There's no war, dear sir, is there?

—What do you mean, there's no war?

—That's the trick, indeed. He-he. Pure *magique.*

—Listen to me,—says the thought and switches to a whisper.—It's only "pretend". Poof!

It makes a magician's gesture, the war disappears, and a cloud of its remnants flies away.

—*Magique!*

—Pretend? Oh...

—Pretend, exactly,—the thought sips from its skull-cup and continues.—It's merely a pre-emptive counter-military peacekeeping operation or a small local conflict somewhere out there on a neighbouring island, if you prefer that. What kind of war is it?

—Ahhh...

—Sounds strangely "unwarly", pardon me.

—Ohhh... I see.

—This semantic wordplay of yours sometimes renders me ecstatic,—says the thought and fakes shivers.

—And it is intended, incidentally, to end the war (and all wars, by the way) and thus to complete the assembly of utopia in our Novo Tsarstvo.

—Just like that.

—Sometimes it's easy to forget about what it's all for.

—This is another important semantic feature of

our Novo Tsarstvo. You see, we don't start wars; we end them. Poof!

—More like "bang!".

—Indeed, dear sir, our Novo Tsarstvo is brimming with all sorts of such features.

The thoughts chuckle collectively.

—Peculiarities!

—What an amusing wordplay!

—Indeed, we have plenty of wonders to chew on.

—Chew on whatever you like, as any true utopia should be, shouldn't it?

—Uh-huh!

—So, we must drink to that, don't you reckon?

—Oh, indeed!

—Well, now we're talking!

—A toast! Someone?

—A good toast, we need a good toast!

One of the thoughts stands up. Silence. The thought clears its throat and begins:

—We're lucky to live in a country where at times one cannot help but marvel.

—Huzzah!

—Huzzah!!

—Huzzzzzah!

The thought that huzzahed first throws the cat skull on the floor; it shatters into jagged fragments that scatter around the room. Hundreds of other thoughts, whether they have participated in the dialogue or remained silent, empty their cups in one go and smash them too, asynchronously. The noise of cracking bones turns into a roar of a water cascade that rings and hums in our ears, intensifying until

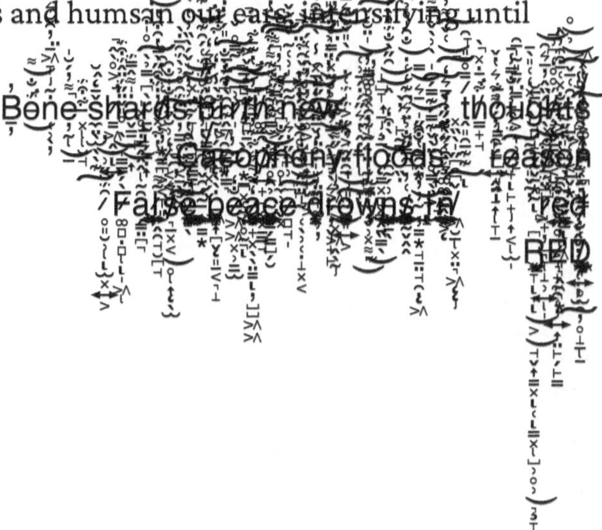

With the accompaniment of deafening tinnitus, the white starkness around us begins to move, rippling and shimmering like the surface of snow amidst a field touched and soothed by the wind, and upon it, as if it's an inkblot test, faceless figures surface and commence a dialogue:

—Imagine that the world exists simultaneously in several permutations and they arise from spontaneous and diverging developments.

—Uh-huh.

—Suppose, for example, if one stays at home instead of going to the shop, this too can trigger a chain of events such that, in one version, it could change the world. Imagine, when en route to the shop, you might fall in love with someone, start a family, raise children, and the children could become brutal dictators who would devastate the planet by exchanging a volley of nuclear warheads, but if you had stayed at home, this would not have happened.

—Makes total sense.

—No, it fockin' doesn't! It doesn't! Bullshit! Bullshit! Total crap! Shut up! Shut up!

—That's a little bit saccharine... Just a tiny bit too much, if I may.

—By your logic, they also can become benevolent rulers who propel the arts and sciences, leading us all to the promised utopia, couldn't they?

—That's precisely true, but my point is, the set of such probabilities and outcomes is infinite, and nothing is impossible within its boundless realm. In one of the strata where we live, for example, Novo Tsarstvo, formed from the ruins of the erstwhile Velika Imperia, there are endless special military operations, asymmetric warfare, national unity under a strong leader, patriotism awareness campaigns, information security and media regulation, education reforms and mental hygiene, economic challenges, discipline enforcement and order maintenance, privacy protection and security monitoring, social harmony, and other political and semantic features of our noble regime, as if someone had cranked it up to the limit.

—Or artistic expression, emotional engagement, stability, and well-being!

—This is exactly where I'm getting at. At the same time, somewhere, there is a reality that is just like ours, but where those things are called by their names. Such as "war" is called "war", or, on the contrary, perhaps it has never even existed as a concept! Somewhere there is one reality where what they show on TV and tell in the newspapers is Truth, not even in the sense that our leaders are lying (how could we even assume that?), but in the sense that the fantasies of our leaders may also be real in one of the infinite variations of our reality.

—Woah! A banger, that one. A certified banger. We should frame it, that one, shouldn't we?

—In another one, however, everything is even worse—there is an evil professor who bred a particular breed of *Homo demonicus*, and half of the populace "evolved" into it, and everything flashed red, including the sky, and the sky started laughing. In another one, where everything is the polar opposite, where our archipelago never existed, hence no Velika Imperia, and no Novo Tsarstvo, where the world's geography is completely different, where all the people are happy, lives a person who could somehow be reading our mind right now.

—Bullshit! Outright poop tornado.

The thought starts banging on the table. *Bang-bang-bang* it goes, louder and louder, until some of the thoughts put their hands over their ears.

—Don't freak us out! Please! Don't do that!

—One wishes to know which reality is which. Ha-ha!

—Bullshit! Bullshit!—screams one of the thoughts covering its ears.

They pause, and around them, in a few strokes, the ink paints a dark room, the far wall of which is adorned with a barred window transmitting the dim light illuminating the thoughts' silhouettes.

—Don't you think there's something a little... odd... as if from the Evil One?

—There's definitely a world where the Evil One himself waters the flowers in the morning and plays with the kittens in the afternoon, whether it's in his basement or not, and all is well between them, no harm done.

—It's a pity that that reality isn't ours.

—Absolutely a pity.

—The realities have collided, mixed together, as if at one moment something in the universal mechanism rumbled and clicked, one little cog went off, and many separate strata began to coexist in one. The environment remained the same, but an inflamed fissure, one shared by all, emerged in people's minds. The tectonic plates of consciousness have ripped open, and there is nothing and no one to fill the gaping hole between them.

—Just build a bridge.

—Who can build such a bridge?

—Builders. Bridge builders.

—Where have you seen such builders?

—Architects? There are universities that produce such people.

—Produce?

—Yes. The whole production pipeline.

—Some people have the extraordinary ability to

see many realities; some even manage not only to see them but to switch between them, while most people are destined to live in only one.

—Is this a fantasy novel to you?

—Others think that it is possible to make a pact with these realities to ignore one another to the exclusion of any outburst of mutual interest. Consider us, for example; we have accustomed ourselves to ignoring the television reality, or rather we have accustomed ourselves to thinking so, and we were quite sure that she would also ignore us in return. Seemingly, all should be fine; no one bothers anyone, everyone lives in their own stratum, but then you suddenly notice that someone has fucked you over, hard and completely unscrupulously, mayhaps even with a baton, and at some point, the television reality comes to your door and

Knock-knock

We approach the door, embrace its cold handle with our trembling, dry palm.

—Greetings, I am the television reality,—says the gentle and friendly high-pitched voice.

There she is, in official, militaristic, dark grey attire: a shirt, a skirt, both tweed, heeled shoes, black, polished; in her hands, a leather folder packed with documents; instead of her head, a miniature TV with two telescopic antennae, a slightly cracked screen, and nothing broadcast on it.

We say:

—I don't want to speak about our Lord.

She replies:

—From now on, I'm going to live with you.

—What? Who are you?

—I am the television reality, silly, but you may address me as TVR. It's quite a delight to finally meet you!

She wiggles her antennae.

—Well, I don't feel like it. Go away. You're unwelcome here.

—I must say, your deafness rather amuses me. There appears to be a misunderstanding, silly.

—And what is it?

—Now I live with you.

She smiles, and her antennae grow.

—Very funny,—we reply, shaking our head.

She stops talking and examines the surroundings.

—It's a bit chilly out here on the landing. Blood on the floor. The lift, too, is on the blink. Why don't we drop the pretence, and you can invite me in, love?

We shake our head even more.

—I'm not inviting you anywhere. Please. Leave.

We try to close the door, but the TVR inserts her elegant foot into the gap.

—It wasn't a request.

—Leave. Or I'm calling the police. That's an intrusion. Illegal, that.

—Oh, do not trouble yourself, love. The decision has been made at the highest echelons.

She points upwards with her index finger.

—Where?

—Such is the order of things.

—It's absurd.

—Oh, silly, I am fully aware. Please, open the door; don't be so dramatic.

№1.3: Embrasure

The world is collapsing, thousands tortured and killed, and we are making an omelette at three at night. The crackling oil sings in unison with crackling hearts. Suddenly the oil sizzles and splashes, hitting our skin. We scream, jerk our hand back and drop the spatula. TVR shakes her telly-head and lowers the flame on the hob.

Living together with someone is lovely, isn't it?

Most of the day, she hangs around our flat observing us, holding a leather folder and black pencil in her ashen, skeletal hands. From time to time, she seductively licks its graphite tip and writes something down. Perhaps she records what we watch, listen to, do and eat, including the omelette with possibly expired ham.

Perhaps she records what you think, too?

Impossible.

In our small studio, there's nowhere to hide from her, apart from the loo—a newfound sanctuary. Even sitting there, we feel her silent presence behind the door and thankfully note the absence of a spyhole. Sometimes she looms over us, examining how we lie on bedding in the corner near the dining table (our bed is occupied by her) and read or squeeze our head between headphones, listening to wireless news from another stratum of reality about strategic aerial interventions involving explosives performing kinetic precision strikes (or bombing, or shelling), enhanced interrogation techniques and coercive persuasion methods (or torture), irreversible justice delivery (or executions)—none of which are broadcast on the telly. We're unsure if she's aware of what radio channels we tune into and what the hosts tell us because even if we lie still, embracing the radio and pretending to sleep, we can hear her pencil scratching paper. Sometimes it's louder than anything else. Occasionally, she watches us frying eggs or cooking porridge with water and a pinch of sugar, cautioning us not to overcook it or advising care with our fingers when dismembering a year-old frozen chicken.

—First, lay the chicken on a clean, flat surface,— she says smoothly.

Her caring guidance annoys us. We don't want to

wait for her instructions and hurry. The knife slips and cuts our hand, leaving a long trail of blood on the cutting board and chicken. Cold tap water soothes the pain.

—Start with the wings. Find the joint where the wing connects to the body. Carefully cut through the joint and set the wing aside. Repeat this step with the other wing.

That was elementary. Dismembering 101.

—Next, move on to the legs. Like with the wings, find the natural joint between the thigh and body. It should give way easily, if you've found the right spot.

Well done.

—Repeat with the other leg. Now, the breast and back. Cut along the spine, keeping the knife close to the bone. This should leave you with two halves.

Very good! You're a born butcher.

—Lastly, split the breast down the middle, and you should have two separate pieces. You can do the same with the back if you wish. And there you have it —a fully dismembered chicken.

There you have it, a fully dismembered chicken covered in your own blood. You should've listened to her from the start, silly.

—Remember, practice makes perfect, so don't be discouraged if you don't get it right the first time,— she finishes, a grin illuminating her screen.

We try to ignore her and walk around the house as if she doesn't exist—this is the easiest part, for it's not new to us at all. When we collapse into an old and dusty armchair to watch the telly, she stands like a watchtower next to us, observes, and comments. If the telly malfunctions and statics, she comes over and gently adjusts the two long telescopic antennae, just like hers. If that doesn't help, she slaps the telly with her hand, the static disappears, and she says "lovely", softly caressing the telly before returning to her position next to us.

After a certain period of cohabitation, she has started turning the telly on in the early morning and turning it off late at night, keeping it running during the day. If we try to turn it off, she waggles her index finger, turns the telly back on again, and scribbles something in her notebook. Thus, the telly broadcasts incessantly throughout our slumbering hours, and perhaps would broadcast even at night, but none of the government channels have anything to say at night.

The telescreen unremittingly exudes effusions of a special life, a mélange of obstinate asininities.

(THE OLD GENTLEMAN in a wig enters the scene.)

OLD GENTLEMAN: Our other "humanist" and, pardon the expression, "equalist" neighbours...

(At the word "humanist", the audience gasps, and at

the word "equalist", they gasp doubly, either with shock or disgust.)

OLD GENTLEMAN: ...have refused to relinquish our plutonium and copium and now are boycotting our economy, whilst they themselves are in the deepest economic crisis. For them, it seems, their—again, please forgive me—made-up "humanist" principles are more important than the well-being of their citizens. At a time when our economy is demonstrating slight negative growth due to external pressures from the United South, they themselves live in absolute chaos, with the population slowly descending into savagery and beginning to conform, as it seems to me, to the level of the Evil One's ideals.

(The audience laughs.)

OLD GENTLEMAN: Now, we have our first guest, a professor of economics and culture. Hello, esteemed professor!

(The picture splits in two, and a rotund man with a pink mug appears on the right side.)

ESTEEMED PROFESSOR: Greetings! Thank you for having me on your splendid show once again.

OLD GENTLEMAN: Of course, distinguished fellow of science, ser. Tell us, what is the situation in the mainland South now?

ESTEEMED PROFESSOR: The situation is

deplorable, to put it mildly. In addition to a noticeable economic decline, quite a severe one indeed...

OLD GENTLEMAN: Oh, indeed...

ESTEEMED PROFESSOR: ...there has also been a cultural transformation affecting even the most basic domestic changes. People are being advised to do less laundry, use fewer household appliances, wash less, and now, one of the recent innovations, dictated among other things by their economic insolvency, is that citizens are being encouraged to eat insects. Packs of worms, flies, and house cockroaches are already available in their grocery shops.

(The audience gasps.)

OLD GENTLEMAN: Don't they even have cockroaches at home and have to go to the shop to buy them?

ESTEEMED PROFESSOR: That's exactly my point. Shocking, isn't it?

OLD GENTLEMAN: Absolutely shocking. Are they prepared to give up their favourite rare steak and *foie gras* in favour of... that? It's hard to believe, dear professor.

ESTEEMED PROFESSOR: Truth is always hard to believe. That's why Truth is Truth. You have to make an effort. For them, it's heralded as an innovation and an achievement of the food industry! You'll be even more astounded to learn that slug tartare is now considered an exquisite delicacy there.

OLD GENTLEMAN: Ugh!

ESTEEMED PROFESSOR: Yes, ugh indeed. I had to try it.

OLD GENTLEMAN: And how was it?

ESTEEMED PROFESSOR: Absolutely unbearable.

OLD GENTLEMAN: Unbearable. How do they endure over there?

ESTEEMED PROFESSOR: Well, it is not what you would call a utopia, that is for sure. Endurance is **our** virtue. Always has been.

(The audience is ecstatic. The old gentleman bids farewell to the professor and invites the next guest, a pallid man dressed entirely in black with short black hair and the countenance of an undertaker. Here follows a fragment of his speech:)

PROPAGANDOID: Our humanist pundits and dissidents are slinging mud in our Novo Tsarstvo, working off the money paid to them by the United South. These dissidents subsist on imperialist money and are pliant puppets to their overseas masters; it is no secret that all so-called "reformists"—the enemies of our state—are financed by the plutocratic imperialists, living off their handouts, and so does anyone who takes to the streets with a banner or makes a snow angel against our ongoing peacemaking operation in Slobodna Zembla. All snow angels are fallen angels!

(While the propagandoid is speaking, the telly shows young people being arrested by the police. The image cuts to the same young people making snow angels in front of the government building, then cuts again to the same young people sitting in the police patrol car, their hands cuffed.)

PROPAGANDOID: Not wanting peace equals wanting war. These elements are the real traitors; they are the spies and scouts of the United South in our country. They wish for the defeat of our army and an immediate attack by the enemy on our sacred island! They have even conspired about how, if anyone invades our great island, they will surrender their homeland at once! Our beloved Tsar and I have already spoken of the surging swell of patriotism that will not allow anyone to play with our country and will never allow treason to be plotted in our home with impunity. For every step of this dastardly betrayal, it will demand retribution with their heads, with the life of a traitor! They are preparing to commit treason, they are preparing to open the borders of our country to terrorists from Slobodna Zembla, they are ready to fling wide the gates to a foreign invader, but they want to portray this treachery as if it were the dark deed of foreign hands! And this they call their supposedly "genuine" patriotism. Their game is exposed! The mask of their perfidy has been torn from their faces once and for all!

(The propagandoid receives a round of applause and disappears. The programme ends, giving way to another one. A pig-nosed general with a rubicund complexion, small black eyes, and protruding ears comes out, standing in front of a black and red flag with a large white bird resembling an angry dove, the flag of Novo Tsarstvo. The dove's claws are empty, outstretched, and it feels like the bird is about to grab at someone's throat.)

PIG-NOSED GENERAL: Today, our troops destroyed one thousand three hundred and fifty-four terrorists, thirty-three tanks, six aircraft, and fifty-seven pieces of combat equipment. After attacks on several of our peacekeepers' positions, smoke reminiscent of flames appeared, prompting a decision to tactically regroup. Thirteen fighters were reported missing; the rest are unharmed and happy. The situation at the front is difficult but not critical. We have already dispatched dozens of combat units and a fully manned battalion of soldiers ready to defend our island.

(On the screen, clattering among the fields, appears a military train transporting a myriad of black tanks with white doves painted on them. The scene cuts to a priest consecrating the tanks by dousing them with holy water.)

JOURNALIST: How are we going to respond to Slobodna Zembla's escalating support from the United South?

PIG-NOSED GENERAL: Armed with the courage and professionalism of our peacekeepers.

JOURNALIST: How long will the mobilisation last?

PIG-NOSED GENERAL: There is no mobilisation as such. We are sending a request to our Tsar for approval to send reserves to the front, but these reserves may need to be replaced at times. Fortunately, this is not required at the moment, but we will inform you as soon as that happens.

(Then follows an interview with the rocket operator who, it appears, is one of those in charge of ensuring the rockets keep hitting the cities and towns of Slobodna Zembla every day. He doesn't resemble an archetypal military man, but more an archetypal scholar of mathematics and physics, a thin intellectual lost within his spacious uniform, wearing slightly tinted spectacles that people often wear in the hope that the light from a computer screen won't scorch their pupils. His skin appears somewhat ruddy with a purplish hint. On his head, there's a beret, as if to conceal something beneath it. Amidst the perpetual senile stream, the fellow makes an impression of someone who has something interesting to say, the significance of which will not evaporate after every sentence, although there's a high chance that the

interview with him, like with everyone else, is fully scripted.)

INTERVIEWER: Why did you decide to become a military man?

ROCKETEER: Well, because this way I can demonstrate my patriotism through actions rather than words, right? Everyone can boast about how much they cherish their motherland and would do anything for it, but what's the point in talking?

INTERVIEWER: That's true. And why a rocketeer specifically, if I may ask?

ROCKETEER: I have been fascinated by geography since I was a child. I remember spreading a map of the entire archipelago on the floor and exploring Novo Tsarstvo and the other islands. In those moments, there was nowhere to tread in our compact flat without stepping on the map, and my mother would always grumble, though she was generally supportive of my hobby. I know all the cities in the archipelago if you fancy a game.

(The rocketeer smiles, revealing gingival embrasures between his upper front teeth.)

INTERVIEWER: Could you describe your day to us, what is your work like?

ROCKETEER: I have to admit, it might seem incredibly monotonous for most people. Some even question, "What type of soldier are you?"

INTERVIEWER: Well, no doubt, they are wrong.

ROCKETEER: Yes, it's rockets that win wars, not bullets any longer.

INTERVIEWER: I concur. So...

ROCKETEER: Most of the day, you have to hunch over maps, radars, typing instructions and coordinates into the computer, always with a radio at hand, waiting for directives or relaying them. Just like that. Once the computer has calculated everything, I ensure the calculations are accurate, press the button, and the rockets soar.

(The rocketeer performs a gesture akin to sending a spoonful of porridge to a child's mouth.)

INTERVIEWER: How precise are your missiles?

ROCKETEER: The calculations are precise, but as for the missiles ... it varies based on the type.

INTERVIEWER: Well, you always hit some target eventually!

ROCKETEER: That's correct. "Say where, and we'll deliver."

(The rocketeer chuckles, so does the interviewer.)

INTERVIEWER: Is it true that Slobodna Zembla is shelling itself?

ROCKETEER: Not Slobodna Zembla, but the terrorists who have taken root there. A military junta. They're the ones shelling.

INTERVIEWER: What if the United South joins those terrorists ...

ROCKETEER: Well, they're already providing them with weapons. Where do you think they got the missiles?

INTERVIEWER: I meant full involvement, direct participation. What if they declare war against us? Would we be able to retaliate then?

ROCKETEER: We have a bomb, a massive bomb, the most bombastic bomb, a device with absolute lethal capacity that guarantees an absolute hit.

INTERVIEWER: "The Peace Bringer".

ROCKETEER: Exactly.

(The rocketeer smiles from ear to ear.)

INTERVIEWER: Will you be guiding it?

ROCKETEER: Oh, no, I don't think so. *(He waves off.)* It's dropped off a plane. *(He nods, nervously.)*

INTERVIEWER: Wow! That's truly fascinating.

ROCKETEER: Fascinating, yes.

INTERVIEWER: Two final questions ... What do you like most about your job?

ROCKETEER: This might seem odd, but I suppose it's the fact that I can be here in Novo Tsarstvo. Even though I'm in the military, you could say I work "remotely", ha-ha. In the evening after work, I can return home, kiss my wife, hug my daughter, open an atlas with her and study the maps. I love maps and all that, and I impart this love to my daughter too. Perhaps she'll grow up to be a rocket scientist as well. It's a straightforward job for a sharp mind. They say that girls are very welcomed there.

INTERVIEWER: Excellent. And what's the most annoying thing about the profession?

ROCKETEER: I suppose it's having to work during the night sometimes.

(An old man from the Novo Tsarstvo Secret Service, NTSS, a general in full dress uniform, decorated with a dazzling array of medals akin to a New Year fir tree festooned with glittering ornaments, stands in front of the podium.)

NTSS GENERAL: We possess reliable information about the presence of weapons of mass destruction in Slobodna Zembla. To prove that, we demonstrate this … *(He shows off a vial with red sludge in front of the audience)*. This is the chemical weapon being developed a few hundred kilometres away from us. Our security agency found out that bio-laboratories supervised by the United South have conducted experiments involving the causative agents of avian influenza, plague, swine fever, anthrax, cholera, tularemia, brucellosis, Northern fever, hantavirus, tick-borne encephalitis virus, leptospirosis, rabies, and other exotic diseases; including, which we have always suspected, even ones capable of altering a man's very sexual orientation. Some say this vial may even turn one into a demon! Tests were conducted by their terrorist government on their own civilians, including women and children. Simultaneously, they have been developing technical means to deliver these combat pathogens to the battlefield, chemicals that will inevitably be used against us on our own land.

In desperate attempts to shorten the interminable day, we collapse onto our mattress and vigorously rest. But sleep evades us. Our mind is busy with itself, with what it has seen, with what it wants to see but never will.

We don our headphones and fire up the radio, tuning into one of the stations where, as we wish to believe, Truth is still spoken and reality takes an entirely different shape—a horrid abomination of hideous monstrosity, a real reality, the one we crave so much.

We want to hear about something gruesome and daunting, something vile and excruciating—a fallen rocket in a playground, executed prisoners, cities and villages wiped out from the map, snowy fields strewn with unidentifiable bodies, rivers of blood mixed with dirt and snow. It's not a pursuit for escape but its opposite—a wish to be there at the core of it, to hurl ourselves on the sharp edges of Truth and suffer at least the smallest portion of real agony.

We hold out hope for something even worse, something capable of bringing an abrupt end to it all, so endful that even nothingness itself would cease to exist. Yet, there are no new reports, no broadcasts, no static noise. Instead, there, a soothing, serene symphony plays—a lullaby whose composer and title are obscure to us, but we're sure we've heard it some-where; so sure, it feels as if we wrote it ourselves, sent it to the radio station on an old tape, then forgot about it, and now after all those years, it has found us.

A gentle melody emanates from the piano keys, summoning a wistful nostalgia. The left hand marks a consistent rhythm that guides the right hand in a graceful waltz. The music swells, flooding our ears with numerous notes and chords, weaving a tapestry of sound as rich and lush as a summer meadow. It then veers into a minor key, injecting a drop of bitter-ness, grows expressive, twists and turns, brimming with chromatic unpredictability and blasting crescendos.

The piano bids **goodbye** with a soft and delicate touch, leaving behind a **faint** trace of emotions—a beauty birthed from bitterness, recedes and returns to its original theme, **looping** in the melancholy. Yet, there's an unsettling peculiarity to it—as if a single key in the upper register fails to sound, inducing **discomfort** in the listener, causing you to miss a heartbeat, and leaving behind the dense lingering **echo** of

You are in the long corridor where all the bulbs have died. Doors flank it, all shut. A distant drip-drop titillates your ears. A draught tickles your toes. The same symphony resonates from a door nearby. You approach it, press your ear to the keyhole, confirming that the music originates from within, and pull at the handle—it creaks open.

Inside the white room, a grand black piano presides, and on its lid dangles a red skipping rope without handles. Behind the instrument, raised on stools, a duet of a boy and a girl plays the symphony. The girl, with pigtails and wearing a white dress, sits on the left; the slick-haired boy in a white suit and a red bow tie sits on the right. As they see you, the boy and the girl offer a gentle glance and bestowing smile, yet continue to play, uninterrupted. Careful to minimise the creaking, you close the door, return to the corridor, and again shuffle towards the bright light.

At the corridor's far end, a cold, luminescent light emanates, and you see

Truth.

She shrugs off her garments, and the light behind her, playing with abstractions, illuminates her naked and nonchalant silhouette.

She's indescribably beautiful. She lures us to follow. We open our mouth and

Shhh! Don't say anything. Just follow the light.

Oddly, the symphony persists as you distance yourself from the children's room and traverse the corridor Truthward.

We wish we had a body like hers.

You'll never have a body like hers.

Suddenly, the right adjacent door to Truth comes off its hinges. TVR walks out from it, heels clattering. Immediately, she assaults Truth with her bare knuckles. The panicking light behind them starts flashing. You hear grunts and growls, squint, and try to see what's happening. Fending off a few blows, Truth lunges at TVR, forces her to the floor, fists flailing. TVR defends herself with elbows, seeking to dislodge her opponent.

The piano keeps conjuring the symphony. All other sounds cease. The light brightens, transforming the brawling figures into two silhouettes, akin to dancing marionettes in a shadow play.

Abruptly, TVR wrestles back control, throwing Truth off, and retrieves a garrotte from her pocket, crafted from red skipping rope handles and a piano string, and commences the throttling.

Truth flails desperately, grasping at TVR's hands, legs convulsing in a futile struggle, but after several agonising moments of breathless resistance, Truth is quietly quelled.

From atop the vanquished body, TVR rises, a seasoned assassin. She surveys the indescribably beautiful corpse for a moment before turning her gaze towards you.

Frozen mid-corridor, you are paralysed, devoid of resistance.

With exaggerated patience, TVR advances, her footsteps echoing in the silence. She reaches your position and, from her pocket, produces a syringe. The needle pierces your arm, and in an instant, you sense the red sludge silently seeping into your vein, its icy touch spreading through your body.

№1.4: Luft

—Dear friends, citizens of Novo Tsarstvo,— resounds the Tsar's voice from the telescreen and pauses for a few seconds.

Wherever in the room we are at that moment, his pinprick pupils stare out at us, penetrating our soul like the haunting gaze of an old portrait, as if possessing the certainty that the soul truly exists and ensuring it is wholly at his command. His round head is grey, almost bald, with a little scar on his cheek. He's a little, shrivelled, feeble, frail.

Like a desiccated scrotum.

He rasps like a clogged hoover, coughing when his throat dries. His pale, vein-mottled hands fidget restlessly with a biro. His eyes, pools of icy indifference and bottomless apathy, have exiled kindness—a rogue element—to the deep wrinkles in their corners.

Even in silence, his lips move, as if casting spells of mind control.

When you see and hear him, it feels like you're eating porridge made from crushed flies. Each unchewed insect becomes harder to swallow, wedging in your throat and tickling your gullet until your swallowing muscles fail to contract, your air-starved lungs clench in terror, and beads of cold sweat dew on your blue face.

—I come before you today with a heavy heart to discuss our homeland, Novo Tsarstvo, and the collective hardships we face. In these challenging times, the safety of our nation, community, and families takes precedence above all else, for it is my main responsibility to you. Our memory is scarred by The Great Coup, a catastrophe that disrupted the peace we once upheld across our archipelago. That was a dark time: families shattered; chaos reigned. Together, we pledged to remember, to learn, and to never let such a disaster strike again.

He punctuates his speech with thought-chasms, creating a sensation of silence for a fraction of a second. Each time, reality cracks, allowing us to slip from its grasp. A pleasant—nay, narcotic—sensation.

We have always wondered about and questioned the purpose of these pauses, pondering whether they add weight to his words or help him keep pace with the teleprompter, its script written by an alumna of a literary faculty from the University of Quasi-Liberal Arts who once aspired to become the greatest writer of her generation but now finds herself crafting speeches for the elites and the Tsar himself. Or perhaps it's mercy, little empty time between words created to help us better digest his thick, rhetorical substance.

A lurid dream there was of the Tsar living in a bunker surrounded by a horde of doppelgängers, who, condemned for eternity to an endless battle over the place to be the Tsar's next avatar or suck his sceptre.

What if today it's one of them? What if he's terminally ill or no longer alive? Like blue cheese, it's hard to tell whether he's already spoilt or not. Or what if he's a mechanised puppet?

Yes, a marionette manipulated by a dozen people, voiced by a long-languished theatre actor held captive in the depths of the bunker, and all of this is one prolonged, preposterous puppet show with ordinary people as spectators in a boundless sphere of a room on the other side of the camera, the audience bombarded with signs dictating when to laugh and when to weep, when to enable patriotism, exalt our rich history, praise our distinctive culture, despise our enemies, marvel at our bright future, and mourn for all that unattainable past, resenting the rest of the world.

—Times have changed, the world has changed, but the thirst for peace remains unquenched. Today, our peace is under threat, a shadow looming over our neighbouring island, Slobodna Zembla, where a relentless terrorist junta, propped up by the imperialist influences of the United South, asserts its anti-human rule, creating hazards and setting snares, attempting to sway our former allies against us, using innocent lives as mere pawns in their twisted game of world domination. Slobodna Zembla has now become a festering wound on the flesh of our great archipelago and, despite all our trials, the wound refuses to heal, leaving us with no choice but to act, to safeguard our homes and our people. Even now, with the ongoing peacekeeping operation, our brave soldiers face grave risks, defending on the frontlines against the terrorists, trying to cauterise the wound, and now, we find ourselves on the brink of a monumental, pivotal moment, poised to end our special military operation and save our blood from being spilled with a decisive act—a show of force that will put an end to the aggression against us, that will silence the chaos and bring order. To shield Novo Tsarstvo, we will deploy our groundbreaking instrument, "The Peace Bringer"—a powerful weapon that will pacify Slobodna Zembla and secure the tranquillity of our island and the entire archipelago, an act of defence, of protection, an action we must undertake as the stalwart guardians of peace, putting an end to the unrest, to the violence, and, most importantly, to the looming threat against our beloved motherland. May the dove on our flag soar high once more, and may peace reign supreme. Stand strong, Novo Tsarstvo, for we shall not falter—we stand united for our Motherland, we stand resolute for our future!

At that very moment, the Tsar awkwardly attempts a seated bow and vanishes from the telescreen, replaced by the unfurling black and red flag of Novo Tsarstvo with the white dove; the national anthem blares: two orchestral blasts followed by the menacing rhythm of thunderous drums in unison with the tubas and the discordant squeaking of strings in the background, almost immediately joined by a choir ululating about the sacrosanct heritage and preordained triumph over enemies. Instead of standing up while the anthem plays, we are dragged downwards, our legs like liquefied lead, the bones vanished, the muscles disentangled. The anthem ends.

—It's 6:15 am in Novo Tsarstvo. The mild winter has come to a close. Today will begin bitingly, with temperatures around minus 30 degrees Celsius in the morning, but as the day progresses, the sun will shine and the temperature will claw its way up 5 degrees by noon before plummeting once more, the atmospheric pressure remaining relatively high at about 1040 hectopascals. Blustery winds from the north are expected throughout the day, reaching speeds of up to 20 kilometres per hour, which may further intensify the biting chill, with possibilities of flurries in the evening and at night. Residents should exercise extreme caution on the roads due to the insidious black ice, particularly treacherous at intersections and turns, and remember that we are entering the enchanting season of the Northern Lights, seeking out open spots with minimal light pollution for the most breathtaking viewing experience. Be careful and remember to bundle up!

Ludicrous music starts to play. Two individuals appear at the table. They greet the audience, each other, and then launch into an animated gossip.

In the violent paroxysm of cowardly fever, a sullen thought invades our brain and courses through our body with a revolting sensation, forcing us to seize the telly, drag it to the window, stammering, panting, rip the cord out of the socket (or the entire socket, no reason for it to remain) and hurl the black box from our thirteenth floor straight down to the pavement. Perhaps nothing else would happen, and the telly, with a broadcast still running on it by sheer inertia, would shatter into a thousand shards of glass and plastic; however, a minor accident might unfold as there would be standing a demonic pigman in a balaclava, waiting for its next victim.

Perhaps, you.

And the telly would land on the demon's head.

Like a bomb, indeed. The balaclava wouldn't save the poor little piggie.

Thirteen floors, approximately thirty-five metres, two and a half to three seconds of exhilarating freefall.

The word is soaring! The word is free!

Like a meteorite, the telly would flash, dragging a tail of wire with a torn-out socket at its end, and, instead of nailing the demon to the Earth, it would lead the demon's utter annihilation—"utter" because it would smash the demon's head, reducing it to a porridge, blood and bones mixed with the shattered glass of the kinescope, merging into one farcical fiasco, a spontaneous art installation.

"The Power of the Word..."

Passers-by would be strolling along, sneaking furtive glances at the unsettling spectacle, adjusting their collars and straps of their rucksacks and bags, burying their gloved hands deep in their pockets, then averting their gaze, looking forward or down, some-where at a forty-five degree angle, so they would see nothing but a few metres of treacherous surface in front of them, scurrying away from the scene before they dissolve into the depths of the cityscape, their worn soles polishing the slippery road for future generations to come.

We, meanwhile, would remain upstairs, teetering on the edge of the open window, buffeted by the biting wind, gulping, and then we would vomit everything we have inside us and send it raining down to the pavement to complete that spontaneous art installation.

Stop using 'would', would you? You're already in the thick of it. Comprehend the gravity of what has just happened. Feel the atmospheric pressure dropping around you. Sprint to the bathroom, barricade yourself inside, perch on the sacred porcelain throne, and wait.

Wait for what?

Your ears buzz, your thoughts flutter against the soft walls in your head, chirping and giggling, stumbling and falling down. Look in the mirror. Your mother's best creation. Pure accident, as everything is.

It should have been broken.

It is. It is cracked, see? Fissures are everywhere in the surrounding space, decorating it like a spider's web. Pale, sinister, with tangled locks of greasy hair clinging to the face. She used to say you were pretty, didn't she? The murderer, the vigilante, the peace-bringer, the one who delivered the preemptive blow. Pull your lower eyelids down, upper eyelids up. Look inside the pupils. See? There, in the depths of the black dots, consciousness still resides. You see it, and it sees you back. Say 'Hi', would you?

Hi.

Grab your hair, pull it out in strands, run out of the toilet, peer out of the window, and look again at what you've done. Remove the carpet from under the armchair, roll it, take a bucket with a dustpan and a small broom, and head for the lift.

This life isn't working.

"This lift"?

That isn't working either.

Then what's working for you now is an intangible spiral of steps and phantom railings that will guide you down.

Thirteen floors. Two-point-seventy-five metres per floor. Seventeen centimetres per step.

Your heart, like a jackhammer, punches a hole in the ability to act ~~sensibly, reasonably, deliberately~~

There's a luft between the body and mind.

One, two, three, four, five, six, seven, eight, nine, ten, eleven, twelve, thirteen

Make friends with your limbic system. Run!

fourteen, fifteen, sixteen, seventeen, eighteen, nineteen, twenty, twenty-one, twenty-two, twenty-three, twenty-four, twenty-five, twenty-six, twenty-seven, twenty-eight, twenty-nine, thirty, thirty-one, thirty-two, thirty-three, thirty-four, thirty-five, thirty-six, thirty-seven, thirty-eight, thirty-nine, forty, forty-one, forty-two, forty-three, forty-four

Breathe, control your breathing.

Who are you, an elderly?

thirty-seven, thirty-eight

Wait-wait-wait-wait-wait you've been there already you've fucked it up

                        we don't care

             we can't count now

          we can't do anything

                        keep the fucking count!

thirty-nine, forty, forty-one, forty-two, forty-three, forty-four. Thirty forty-five, forty-six, forty-seven, forty-eight, forty-nine, fifty, fifty-one, fifty-two, fifty-three, fifty-four, fifty-five, fifty-six, fifty-seven, fifty-eight, fifty-nine, sixty, sixty-one, sixty-two, sixty-three, sixty-four, sixty-five, sixty-six

                        breathe, breathe!

sixty-seven, sixty-eight, sixty-nine, eighty, eighty-one, eighty-two, eighty-three, eighty-four, eighty-five, eighty-six, eighty-seven, eighty-eight, eighty-nine, ninety, ninety-one, ninety-two, ninety-three, ninety-four, ninety-five, ninety-six, ninety-seven, ninety-eight, ninety-nine, one hundred, one hundred one, one hundred two

> you don't have to say "one" every time

hundred three hundred four hundred five hundred six hundred seven hundred eight hundred nine hundred ten, hundred eleven hundred twelve, hundred thirteen

> you don't have to say "hundred" either
> there isn't much left

fourteen, fifteen, eighteen, nineteen, twenty twenty-one twenty-two twenty-three twenty-four twenty-five twenty-six twenty-seven

> degrees of pain in the left side of the
> ribcage and

twenty-eight one two one two

is your drill march killer march

thirty thirty-one thirty-two thirty-three run for your
life thirty-four thirty-five thirty-six thirty-seven
thirty-eight thirty-nine when is the end

it's near my friend
it's near don't skip the numbers
would you

forty one hundred forty-one forty-two forty-three
forty-four forty-five forty-six forty-seven forty-eight
one hundred forty-eight
that's it!

no it's not

forty-nine fifty fifty-one-two

it's you, it's your fault!

no no no   no   no
it's not us
it's not even the telly
(an object in freefall)

that destroys

(turns the demon's head into a porridge)

in the case of the falling
what destroys is
the impact force when one object
(the telly)
collides with an obstacle
(the demon)

we (what is "we" even?)
have nothing to do with that
we have nothing to do with it at all

yes you do!
of course you do!
they're coming for you already!
you think you can porridge a pig
on the pavement and get away with it?

yeah!
yeah absolutely!
it's all surface elasticity
(the pig's head)!

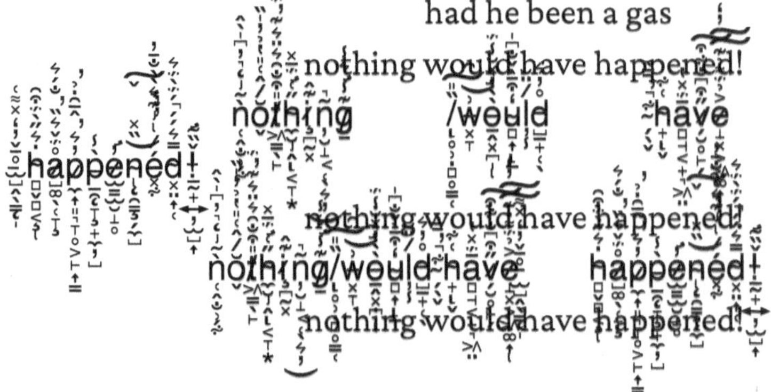

had he been a gas
nothing would have happened!
nothing /would have
happened he would have blown apart and
thanked us for the tickle wouldn't've he would have
blown /apart /and thanked us for the tickle
wouldn't've he would have blown apart
/and thanked us for the tickle
wouldn't've the pig's /head /nothing
would've happened nothing!
head HEAD HEAD
HEAD
HEAD
HEAD
HEAD
HEAD
HEAD

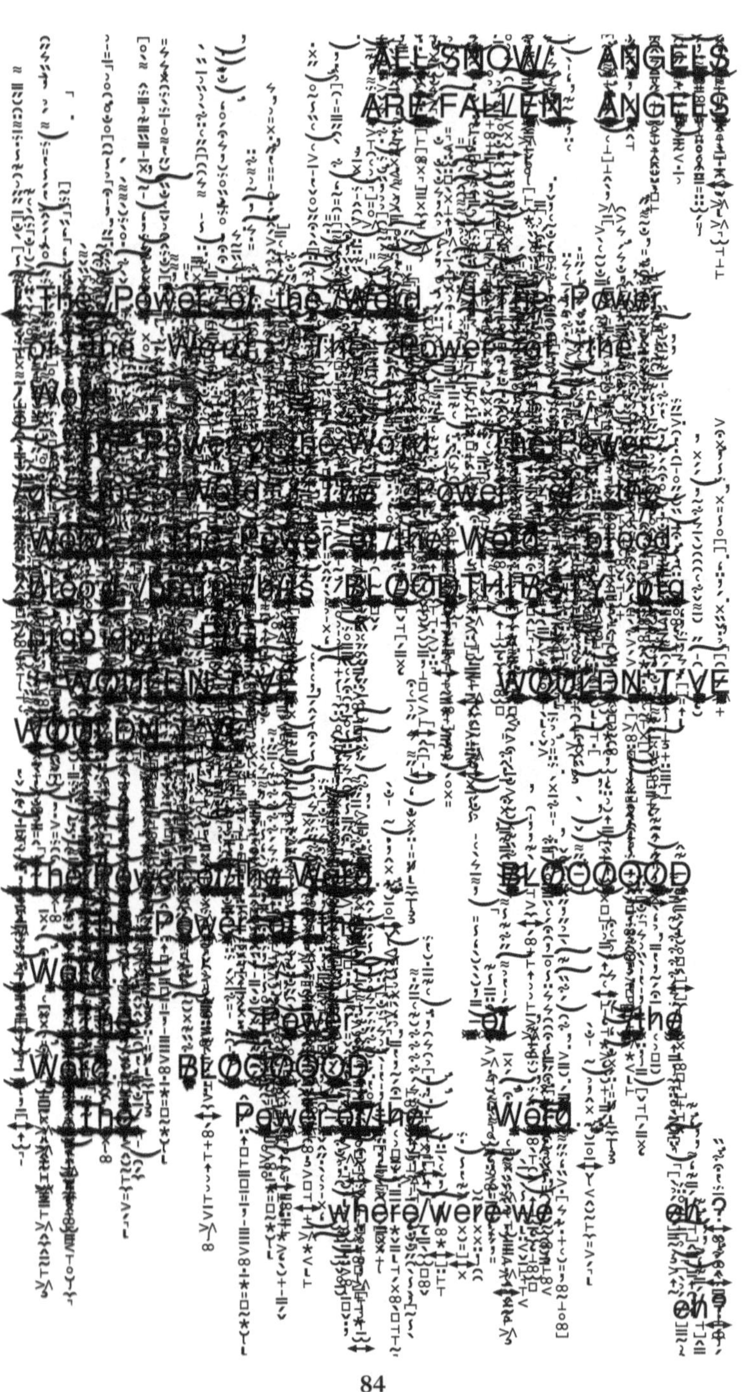

84

where were we, eh?

ALL SNOW ANGELS
ARE FALLEN ANGELS
The Power of the Word   The Power
of the Word   The Power of the
Word
The Power of the Word   The Power
of the Word   The Power of the
Word   The Power of the Word   blood
bloody BLOODTHIRSTY bla
blah blah blah
WOULDN'T VE
WOULDN'T VE
The Power of the Word   BLOOOOOOD
The Power of the
Word   the
Power   of the
Word   BLOOOOOD
The   Power of the   Word
where/were we

sixty-seven sixty-eight-nine seventy seventy-one-two-three-four-five-six-seven-eight-nine-ten-eleven

eighty it should be eighty you dimwit!

eighty eighty-one-two-three-four-five-six-seven-eight-nine-ten

ninety say it in full again you're fucking it up again you cunt

one hundred ninety, one hundred ninety-one, one hundred ninety-two, one hundred ninety-three, one hundred ninety-four, one hundred ninety-five, one hundred ninety-six, one hundred ninety-seven, one hundred ninety-eight, one hundred ninety-nine

two hundred

YES!

two hundred and one two hundred and two

we're closer than ever
closer to the bottom of
this enormous boundless pit
two hundred three
two hundred four

the **bottom**

the bottom can you **feel it?**

can **you?**

it's **cold**

it's so cold

two hundred **five**

two hundred **six**

two **hundred   seven**

here here jump over **the last/ three**

A lurid dream there was of a quiet early morning, still dark. The useless street lights flickered drearily. The snow fell perpendicularly, cushioning the pavement and the deserted street. No sound heard. No passer-by seen. No one, not now at least. They may had scampered, possibly hidden, lurking, waiting, questioning themselves, wondering what was going to happen to that marvellous art installation and who that ingenious artist that made it was.

Except it wasn't and it isn't a dream, silly.

Someone stabs us from inside under the rib.

Welcome, breathlessness.

Cold air wheezes in our throat before it has time to warm up in the nose and mouth

You shouldn't have skipped gym class to go to the library. You should have run, run, run, learned to breathe, mastered the motion of your limbs, for life is unpredictable. You never know what a television dropped on a demon from a thirteenth-floor might do to it. Look icy pavement, here it is, splayed out, still resembling a human body. Its head is a gory disaster. The television sometimes can truly be mind-blowing!

Please stop.

Around the demon, the blood covers the icy pavement. The snow is crimson. Pieces of brain, bones, the glass and plastic left from the broken television are all scattered around.

With the rolled carpet under our arm and the bucket in hand, we approach it but slip on the blood-moistened ice and plummet onto the body. Under the dark clothes, it's probably still warm.

An eyeball is floating in the puddle of filth, see? It sees you.

We use our dustpan and broom, scoop up the installation.

Hurry!

Our hands are shaking. The bloody slush is splashing. Our pupils keep dilating. Our mouth keeps drying out.

You forgot to put on your shoes, silly.

Is that an ear?

Collect as much as you can and hide the large pieces in the snowdrift. The rest will freeze into the pavement by dawn, covered with snow. No one will notice.

It is snowing...

Thank snow, do it.

Thank you, dear snow.

Good.

Passers-by will only think that some drunkard was walking home with jingling bags again, slipped, fell face-first on the ice, split his lip, nose, or his eyebrow and bled on the road.

What a disgrace! Put that horn in your pocket. Roll

out the rug. Drag the bloody body onto it, wrap it up. You used to enjoy rolling yourself up in the carpet when you were a child, using this same carpet and pretending you were a mummy. Your dear parents were grudging, but each time you did that, after a minute or even less time you had a sudden urge to leave the carpet-chamber, realised that you couldn't do it, and your claustrophobia kicked in, leaving you believing you would stay inside the carpet forever and end with a dreadful demise within the rug. You started screaming for help, crying, and your parents, laughing lovingly, unwrapped you.

Remember?

Now, it's your turn to wrap and unwrap. Hang the bucket full of demonic leftovers onto your shoulder, turn your back to the entrance, grab the head end of the carpet.

But aren't we supposed to bring a body inside legs-first? Isn't that how it's always done?

Do you want to smear the entire building in blood, silly? Grab the body. Up, up only. It's not too heavy. Perhaps the head was the heaviest part. Press the lift button with your nose.

This lift isn't working.

Up, up only!

Those thirteen floors again through the dark stair-case littered with cinders and butts and condoms and cans, newspapers and needles, smelling musty, smelling of damp and dust, smelling of human filth.

Time goes by in arithmetic progression. One... two... four... eight.

Stop doing that. Drag the body. Don't think about anything. Turn off your mi

—Is that blood?

It's her, the old lady, your neighbour, her nose broken and blue. It's the thirteenth floor.

Your physique is impressive. Good work

We're alone with her in the stairway.

Yes, this is where it ends.

A heavy lump goes down your throat.

Please, say something.

No, you must say something

—Erm, yes... We... we... cut our hand while preparing frozen chicken.

Pause. She stares at us, not blinking, then frowns.

—You should've defrosted it, love, don't you know?

Pause. We swallow.

—Ugh, we know but... we didn't have time for defrosting. Thank you, though.

Nod and smile.

No, creepy, you look creepy. Stop smiling.

Concerned, she scans us from top to bottom.

—You look ill. Are you eating well, love?

Her gaze is concentrated on the bucket.

—Not really, ma'am. Just erm—

—What's in the bucket, love?

Busted. Now you have to kill her, too

—Erm, m-am, it's a porridge... Pig porridge.

She squints with suspicion.

—Pig porridge? Hm—

—Yes, ma'am, indeed. Please, we have to go. We're in a bit of a ru—

—Is it from a pig?

—Yes.

—From a real pig?

—A metaphorical pig, ma'am.

You should've told her it's from a demon. A real demon, a dead demon.

—Uh-huh... A porridge?

—It is, ma'am, a porridge.

She's thinking. Give her some time.

—Porridge from a pig... I don't understand, love.

Unnerving, she is!

—We thought you were a wise woman, but you're asking such silly questions, ma'am.

—Me? Wise woman? Hah, look at me, love. "Wise woman."

Look at her. An old hag who busted you. She is about to call the police. Kill her.

—You're right, you're right... Please, can we go?

Void, the matter-eating void hungry for more emptiness.

—What's floating in there? In your pig porridge.

Tell her the truth. If you don't, no one will

—Television.

—What?

—It's a telly, ma'am, look closely. Shattered.

She does.

—What a nonsense... You're lying to me, love, aren't you?

—No, not at all. We wouldn't dare lying. Never. We want to be like her.

—Who?

—Truth, m'am.

—Ah, *she*... I see... I see...

—It shattered, the telly. We're not lying. We threw it out of our window.

The harder she squints, the less wrinkled her forehead becomes, the further back moves her wig.

—Are you drunk? Are you delirious?

—What? No, we're not. We don't think so.

She notices the boot sticking out of the rolled carpet and starts blinking and rubbing her eyes with the backs of her hands, covers her eyes with her palms and mumbles something.

—Am I delirious?..

—We don't know, ma'am. It may be you, may be us, maybe we've both lived in collective delirium for dozens of years and there's nothing left in the world apart from that delirium in which it's the order of things to flush remnants of a policeman down the toilet, for the order of things is odd. So odd you can't imagine it, ma'am. But we can.

A gentle smile stretches on her face.

Pull one as well. Do it. Squeeze out all the innocence left in you right on your face

—Perhaps we are both delirious.

—Perhaps we both are.

She glances into the bucket, at the carpet, and shakes her head.

—Well... Good luck, love. Please take care of yourself.

—Thank you, ma'am, and you have a lovely day too.

About to turn around, she scratches her chin and asks:

—By the way, why do you refer to yourself as 'we', love?

—Because 'we' are never lonely, ma'am.

The old lady shakes her head, crosses herself, mumbles something, and retreats to her flat, sits by the window, turns on the wireless, listens to the white noise, and melancholically stares into the—

Well, you don't know where, you're not omniscient, are you? You can't see that, she's in her flat now, behind the closed door, probably calling the police.

Your metal door is open so don't wait and burst in

put the bucket on the floor first lock click second lock click then the latch click and now to the toilet to the toilet to the toilet lock yourself in again so no one can see the lid of your porcelain throne is open and ready to take in your creation wholly entirely from your bucket young dissident extremist terrorist murderer pour pour your hellish cocktail your demon brew into the sewer and flow flow the cocktail flow all the way through the pipes but please don't clog them up please. Flush flush flush flush. Oh no, what a fiasco. The water level rises. It's muddy and bloody with pieces of bones and brain floating in it. It's going up. Up, up only. Take the toilet brush and start thrusting the pig porridge down. Your heart pumps blood through your veins into your head with the same vehemence and futility you try to pump down the porridge. You're snivelling, tears teetering behind your eyelids, rolling down your cheeks and raining into the bowl below. The mixture of toilet water, infernal ichor, and your salty drops splashes around, soaking your clothes, running down your face, entering your mouth—an unwelcome baptism in filth and fear. The bowl is still overbrimming. You push the toilet brush far into the siphon. Something cracks and the handle alone remains in your hand while the brush itself rests wedged in the U-bend. You're losing this battle. You're losing to a grotesque slop. You are nothing. An agonised whimper erupts from the dank depths of your gullet. Plunge your hands into the filthy substance and clean the siphon. Don't mind the nausea, your futilely contracting stomach doesn't understand the situation. Moreover, you have nothing to vomit with, you've already been cleansed. Now, do that to the toilet. Uproot the brush, rid all remnants clogging the plumbing, including the bony and the brainy bits, and the incisive shards of the telescreen. It is your ordeal. Let the substance flow! Down, down only. The rhythm of your rushing blood turns into applause, then, for a moment, into silence, until your sob, raw and guttural, shreds it into tatters. You're free, water, please go. Please, water. Please. It does. The water answers to your plea. Don't think, dive into the sink. Behold your reflection in the mirror (young dissident extremist terrorist murderer). Don't cry—it won't help, it will only irritate your eyes. Wash your face, your hair, mop it, twist it in a bun, and drink, drink, drink, drink, drink that chlorinated liquid rich with the flavour of rust and lime. The body! The bo—

Peek out from the toilet. Here she is, your telly-headed mistress, standing there, shaking her telly-head, etching the course of events in her notebook. You've failed her. She's disappointed in you, though it's hard to tell. Her screen shows nothing but your faint reflection.

She will snitch on us.

And hello jail. Because of you.

They will kindly place us against the wall and shoot us. No one will ever know what happened. That will be a good ending.

What about your multiple realities now? How many do you see?

Ignore, ignore, ignore.

No, you can't escape it anymore; you have to choose. You must hide the body.

Fridge? Freezer?

It would only fit a head but there isn't even a head anymore.

A suitcase, our late father's travel suitcase.

Yes, throw his old clothes out of it. Unwrap the demon from the carpet, toss it aside. Lay the suitcase next to it. Shove the demon inside. Close it.

No, no, no, it's not closing. It's not fitting into it.

Put him in the foetal position. The suitcase is a womb and the demon's ready for rebirth.

No, the demon is too large to fit the suitcase. They aren't designed to fit demons, they are designed to fit things.

Turn the demon into things then! Unfold the carpet back and drag the demon to the centre of it. Prepare to butcher.

—Make sure your knife is sharp—a dull knife is a

dangerous tool,—murmurs TVR, suddenly appearing behind you, hovering and whispering,—But better get a saw.

She's very caring again. But "a saw"? We don't have a saw.

Ask your—

knock-knock

—Morning, ma'am.

—Morning again, love. What can I do—

—Have a saw?

—Saw? I didn't see anything.

—No-no, the tool. We need a saw.

—Ho-ho, why would you need a saw at such an early hour? I wonder...

—We ... We ... the chicken is, well ... *gulp* very solid, and our knife is quite dull. It is for dinner.

Her eyes show a hint of curiosity.

—Dinner? At such an hour, love?

—We ... we ... we're hungry, ma'am.

—Oh you, poor thing. I only have a hacksaw, though, love.

—That will do, ma'am.

She claps her hands once and smiles.

—Lovely! You're having a busy morning, aren't

you, love? I can't sleep myself. It must be the weather ... Old bones ... Ho-ho.

She gives you the hacksaw. Bid her a pleasant day again and go back to the demon. On your knees. Look at it, lying here before you, helpless, motionless, vulnerable, its entirety in your power. You can do whatever you want.

Our lungs defy inhalation. We don't know what to do.

—Start with the arms,—says TVR.—Find the joint where the arm connects to the body. Carefully cut through the joint and set the arm aside. Repeat this step with the other arm.

Place the hacksaw on his shoulder and with a frictional movement, back and forth, pull and push, pull and push. You squint as the dark demon blood sprinkles, already cold and stinky. The hacksaw penetrates its skin, to flesh, to bone, as blood spurts out on the carpet. It soaks it all in like a sponge and transforms into a quagmire. Pull and push, pull and push. The red sludge, the demon blood, enters your mouth and—

—Next, let's move on to the legs,—she happily continues.—Like with the arms, find the natural joint between the thigh and the body. It should give way easily if you've found the right spot.

Obey. It takes time, but trust her. Just pull and

push. Don't weep. Why do you keep weeping? No redemption for you, it's been already sold out.

There's nothing else left to do but weeping.

This is who we are now, a weeper; this is where it all ends.

A lurid dream there was of a butcher who sold the demon's flesh to angels. The heavens in that week were short on demon's meat. The angels craved to feast and celebrate their virtuous, righteous, holy nature, and thought they must, and had no other choice but act, unlock the gates of hell and let the demons out and hunt them down.

—Repeat with the other leg.

The demons fled into the night, but all were caught and slain with glee. The butcher carved them with delight and brought them to the angels' spree. They ate the demon flesh and loved the taste of sin, and soon they ran out of their stash and looked for more to feed but couldn't find it, for demons now were extinct. They searched the barren hell, they rummaged through the heavens, until with shock and awe they realised the only demon left to kill was hiding in the butcher's skin.

Too coherent for a dream, isn't it?

—...And there you have it—a fully dismembered body. Remember, practice makes perfect, so don't be discouraged if you don't get it right the first time.

№1.5: Penumbra

As fade the fractals of wild, wicked thoughts, you walk out of the tower block into the drifts, rolling the suitcase behind on a trolley. No path is laid: no icy blood-smeared pavement, no benches, no art installations, only a holey trail early pathfinders left, as if nothing had ever happened. Everything from house to house is shrouded with pristine snow, slightly grey in some places. You've always found yourself alone in the desert, but now it's as vivid as never before. It's already daylight but not for long. Frost is omnipresent, the sort under which it would be better to forget that the street is still fit for life and stay at home, snug in a warm blanket to safeguard your dwelling. Someone shamelessly stole your future and drained all the warmth out of this world. You are the only fragile being in which a fire still burns, ready to extinguish any second.

Around you, everything is white-grey, speckled with black, from the road beneath your feet to the horizon and from the horizon farther back around the planet. You navigate the endless labyrinth of tower blocks, sporadic black trees, and occasional spruces, whose branches sag under the weight of the snow, so they morph into conical extensions of the drifts.

The sand on the icy pavement crunches under your feet. Hunched over, you go on, yet you can't fathom why, where to, or how; you simply go as if your feet carry you of their own accord, as if they have a plan undisclosed to you and know what they're doing. The only destination that matters is someplace far beyond this street, this city, or better still, this island, this planet, this universe.

Please stop the planet; we need to get off.

Shhh, don't speak!

The sun is capable only to dazzle. Its beams reflect and glitter like tiny crystals manifold on the path ahead, on the drifts around, on the windows of houses and cars that pass by emitting faint wisps of exhaust. It's perfect weather to plunge deep into snow, freeze solid, and let the nature conserve you there like a mammoth until spring arrives, the snow melts away, and the cityscape, which in winter appears more like a dusted architectural model, regains some semblance of life again. Near the pavements and under the fences, traces of human existence will sprout: beer cans, small bottles of something stronger, plastic bags, needles, empty cartridges of nitrous oxide, rotten remnants of newspapers and cartons, wrappers from chocolate bars that will never rot or decompose, cigarette butts and empty packs, dog excrement left uncollected, and somewhere amidst all that splendour, your extinct cadaver in fossilised form.

At a bus stop, a few sullen, silent spectres wait, all dressed in monochrome. They puff steam and papirosa smoke, step from foot to foot, transfer their bags from hand to hand, their gaze transfixed on the hazy horizon. Casting a sideways glance, the spectres greet you with indifference, and you all begin your collective wait for the saviour to come.

Your veins freeze even under many layers of clothing: a shirt, a jumper, a coat, underwear, cotton-insulated trousers, woolly socks, fur boots, red mittens, and a hat plus a scarf, also woolly and also red, whilst your face remains bare and all you wish is a balaclava.

The parched air nips at your flushed cheeks, your teeth chatter like a pneumatic drill; eyelashes, eyebrows—all adorned with rime. Through your

cracked lips, plumes of steam billow. Your nose snuf-
fles and runs, each careful breath burning the irritated
nostrils with fire. The tips of your fingers and toes
grow frostbitten, bereft of blood. They pinch, they
tremble, they grow numb, and you rub them against
each other, anticipating that moment when they once
again feel warmth, when hot-as-lava blood surges
through their veins, and you experience a torturous
yet tantalising tickle.

Belching out a trail of foul gas, the coughing diesel
jalopy arrives at the bus stop and sucks the crowd in
like a vacuum. By perfect misfortune, your suitcase
gets stuck in the entry door. Cold sweat trickles down
your spine, and your body shivers. The embittered
spectres judge you as you struggle to drag the suitcase
in. Nobody helps you with it, though you must refuse
help if it comes, for it's your skeleton in your closet,
nobody can help you. With a rumble, you squeeze in,
drop a few coins to the driver, crawl to the back of the
almost empty cabin, and sit.

The bus is as quiet as a catafalque. The clocks on
the other side of the cabin show 88:88. Time has rele-
gated itself to an abstract concept with free interpre-
tation; it's not something that happens to you
anymore; no, now *you* happen to time if you wish.
Everything's so sluggish and slow, and things that do
manage to happen out of non-existence stay with you

forever, piling up, clutching together until the whole world turns into one colossal, clumsy chimerical construct. The monotonous movement and the arrhythmic murmuring of the engine place you into a trance, and you begin to ask yourself questions you'd never ponder and visualise things you'd never conceive. You visualise how a bleak reflection of your face smears over the window and assumes surreal and grotesque forms, and visualise how that mug would blur across the pavement in the same way the demon's face blurred and turned into a crimson puddle of blood, brain, and snow. You visualise again and again how the television flies from your window and hits the demon's head. You visualise your phoenixian fall and rise. You visualise your tears plummeting into the toilet bowl before you flush its contents. You visualise the old lady, her flowered shawl, her grey hair, her mellow, wrinkled face, and her ringed, veined, mottled hands with a hacksaw brought to you. You visualise what the hacksaw did to the demon, its every movement to and fro, every gusher of blood, every cracking bone, every scream that wouldn't've happened if the demon had been alive. You visualise the demon in its present state, inside the suitcase, resting, meditating on what happened to him—snap and done, once and forever.

Where do demons go after they die?

There's nowhere else to go because you are all already where you are supposed to be, together.

Your fellow passengers' faces would make good gargoyles. You can't guess their emotions, and any attempts at mind-reading fail, for there's nothing to guess and nothing to read. It might be because of the news, might be because of the way of life, might be a sum of both. When time turns to ice, so do the reasons for being happy. Your bus mates had always been like that: austere, serious, strained, concentrated, constrained. That slowness dwells within them, in how they blink, in how they move, in how they think, in how they breathe, at times recharging their lungs with stinking, oxygen-poor air, giving themselves a second to relax before they hinder their breath again. You are no different. Such is your demeanour, stoic and reserved.

Does it have something to do with our inherent northernness?

There's no such thing.

With our harsh history?

It has nothing to do with that either.

But—

Shut the fuck up.

But—

You are not in charge anymore.

Bend over the suitcase. Sniff it.

Nothing.

Unzip it a little at the top and look inside—still there, wrapped in plastic bags.

—Don't worry, it'll pass,—a voice appears from nowhere.

You flinch and slowly turn your head to the old man sitting nearby. He's ruddy, bearded and moustached, sparse damp hairs clinging to his forehead. On his lap, he holds a fur ushanka hat. The snow on it has melted, and it looks like a freshly washed cat with the folded ear flaps as thighs. You gulp and look at him again.

—Sorry?

—It'll pass, all I'm saying.

—Will it?

—Don't worry. I was in the same position last month. He wasn't that big, I must say,—he lets out a nervous chuckle.—But the grief was big enough...

—What are you talking about?

—First they die, and you can't keep them out of your head, but then...

The old man sighs deeply and pauses.

—Then what?

—Then they just become good memories, don't they?.. Was it a boy or a girl? How old? You don't have to answer.

—We don't know how old he was.

—Right... Well... You see, people don't give them enough credit. You, for example, you're sad now, I can tell, but before that happened, were you expressing enough appreciation for him? Just think about it, they are the only beings on earth that love us more than they love themselves. Don't they deserve your gratitude and appreciation? A hint of it, at least.

—Do they?

—Oh, they do!

Your hands shake, you gulp again, and utter:

—We don't think they do.

—I'd say even more than any human. We owe them, owe them a lot, aye. Take human speech, for instance—it all started with giving commands, and guess who gave commands to whom?.. Yes, that's right.

Your eyes are blank. The skin on your skull under your red hat creeps to your nape.

—If I could be half the person mine was, I'd be twice as human as I am, you know?

Mute, you keep staring at the old man.

—I'm telling you, youth. Nice suitcase you've got. It's tough to get a proper coffin of that size these days. Expensive as an aeroplane. High demand, they say. I don't think we even make special coffins for them. What a shame, isn't it?

—Special... coffins?

—Coffins, yes. I've always thought we should have cemeteries and bury them properly at least, and I'm not talking about having funerals, processions and all, because people would find it a bit odd, wouldn't they? But just a small ritual, a proper coffin, a place somewhere in the woods, in nature, where they belong.

You look at him and slowly zip the suitcase back up.

—Don't mind my rant, I understand. I just wanted to say you're a good person for doing this, and don't listen to what they say to you—you've got a kind heart, you're doing the right thing. Grieving over a dog is as normal as grieving over a human being.

—A dog?

—A dog, yeah.

—Right.

You rub your eyes and face with your mittened palms.

—It's hot in here, isn't it?

—A bit warm.

—You're not very talkative, are you?

—No, sorry, we're not.

—Who's we?

—We, well...

—No, you don't have to tell me. I get it. Some bonds are very strong.

You nod back, attempt to smile, and say nothing.

Now lean your face against the cold window and watch the drifting drabness and its denizens: how cars pass, how the bus stops and starts again, how people wordlessly hop on and off, how the streets are all the same, and how they lead you through this impregnable order of permanence.

The bus stops once again, and the old man stands up.

—Don't miss the lights, aye?—you hear his voice again and watch as he puts the washed cat on his head.

Say "uh-huh" and nothing else.

—Uh-huh.

The bus approaches Colossus Square, where fuming automobiles run in circles and sequences of fuming humants move from one edge to another. They cross the roundabout when lights turn green and wait in accumulating nervous clusters. Where the square meets the sea lies the broken Colossus, a giant statue with wings made of wires and strings, crashed into limbs and pieces during the Great Coup. Thousands perished during its construction, their bones now resting under the road and pedestrian lane, gradually tamped deeper into the ground by the humants and automobiles above. Now, the fallen giant's remnants remain in the bay to remind everyone of the

bygone greatness and to lure the occasional gawker—
a rare species of tourist.

The bus passes the Colossus's cracked, crowned
head that stands on the pedestal before its ruined feet.
The head stares at you with indifference and a hint of
calcified supremacy. Someone has painted it with red
eyes and a red mouth so it appears as if blood is
leaking from between its cracked lips—cracked from
the cold, of course. Up from the frozen sea juts its fist
with a piece of torch, forever trying to sink yet bereft
of such possibility. Somewhere below the thick layer
of ice, mingling with rocks and seaweed, the rest of
the Colossus rests unburied; time, if it ever unfreezes,
would polish these remnants into simple rocks, and
the future generation, should they happen at all, will
only see his winged shadow covering the city and the
whole island, permanently—like in that lurid dream
where maniac humants weighed the colossus down
and killed him to seize his crown, oversized for them.

Meanwhile, on the square, the Colossus underground station disgorges its humant cargo. They turn
into a thick, gurgling, protoplasmic mass, start
flooding the square, and disperse and merge with the
rest of the crowd. The bus stops at the station, waiting
for the mass to reach it. They rush in from the cold,
they push without forming a queue, they behave like

hungry animals. Some sit beside you, grunting and silently cursing because of the space your suitcase takes up. The bus driver turns on the radio; hissing and intermittently losing signal, it starts broad-casting:

static noise

... the banging voice of peace...

static noise

...our proud natio...

static noise

...Slobodna Zembla has been
    liberated...

static noise

... a righteous and heroic opera...

static noise

...ar. The enemy forces that had occupied and terrorised the city for years...

static noise

... defeated and driven away...

static noise

... vaporised and vanished...

static noise

...lute our brave soldiers and our beloved Tsar...

static noise

... courage and wis...

static noise

... national interests and security...

static noise

...cautionary measures...

static noise

... take iodine pills...

static noise

Cheerful pop music, creating a discordant avant-garde dirge with the static noise, starts playing.

We can't bear it anymore.

Cover your ears with your mittened hands and close your eyes shut, push your palms against your ears, squeeze the eyelids as if they are doors to a bunker, so nothing can penetrate and scratch your senses. Deprive yourself of the outer world.

Reality is irritating.

The canvas, from beige, turns into deep stygian, and your decaying consciousness, spasming in convulsions, starts playing with the silhouettes of objects, their debris and memories, colours and light, forms and shapes, abstract patterns and random noise. The reality, whatever is left of it, hums and pulsates aqueously. For a fraction of a moment, your existence numbs, silence swallows the sound, and then, like a deafening clap in an empty room, your heart reverberates its first beat:

Boo-oo-mmm!

Boo-oo-mmm-m!

Boo-oo-mmm-mm!

Boo-oo-mmm-mmm!

So it hums and rumbles through your head, through your whole body. You can feel the blood, thick red sludge pumping in your ears, the rhythmic drumming growing into relentless crescendo. Your blood pressure spikes, and a thin film of sweat clings to your skin. The seat under you vibrates in tune with the buzzing in your head.

It smells, it still smells, that reality.

The world still has an odour, a taste: old seats that have absorbed the scents of thousands of people, dirt and grime, the sweet metallic scent of rust, diesel and rubber, sulphur, someone's boiled egg, you, your stale clothes. Don't breathe, don't you dare breathe.

We can't, no, our body needs oxygen.

There's not much oxygen anyway.

Are we having a stroke?

You are the stroke that this world's having.

The darkness dances and erupts with black blobs until it becomes all. From the newly established void, a headless man, his clothes covered in blood and pieces of grey matter, appears and, dragging a telly on a wire like a reluctant dog, limps towards you, his every step sounding like a hammer striking an anvil. Perhaps he wants to talk to you, perhaps he wants you to apologise, perhaps he wishes to take you with him to wherever he is now, and thus, his figure growing, he extends his free hand to you and

Stop murmuring. People will stare at you, weirdo. Close your mouth. Squeeze your eyes and ears harder. Think of something nice.

There's nothing nice left.

Nothing? Nothing at all. We are a key of the mistuned grand piano, played by someone who has never touched an instrument and thinks that playing one is as easy as chopping wood.

Meeting oncoming cars, the bus rattles down a wide avenue with bald birches and bushes planted along its perimeter and identical nine-storey grey buildings planted behind them. Ahead is the sun. It had enough time to see what its beloved critters have done to Earth today, so now, blushing with shame and regret, it quietly rolls down to the horizon in front of the bus. Inside the vehicle, there's only you and a few

gulp

demons.

Two of them sit nearby and talk.

Move the suitcase closer to you, put your hand on the handle.

Their skin is dark pink and studded with burst capillaries, their eyes are muddy and red, their fingers are sausages, their—

Don't look at them, and they won't look at you. You can ignore each other; that's easy.

But they are already leering at us. We know what is about to happen. They will ask us why we are staring at them, and we will say that we are not staring at all and just move our eyes here and there, minding our own business; nothing is wrong with that, and the suitcase, we will say to them, contains nothing at all but our deceased dog and the dog only, but such an answer will not satisfy them and will make them deeply convinced that we are plotting something, something evil and malevolent, something that implies a risk to national security, so then they will ask us where we got this suitcase, whether we stole it from someone, and we will answer them, saying, no, this is our own suitcase with our very own very dead dog, ours and no one else's; we haven't stolen the suitcase nor the dog, both were passed down to us by our dear late father. The demons will stare at us, seeing how wretched we are, smelling of fear, fluttering like a moth around a flame, and they won't believe us, and even if they do believe, it won't matter to them. They will sense the odour of dread in the air, the uncertainty in our words, in our shaking head, in our darting gaze, in our twitching hands unable to find a place for themselves, in all our vulnerability which will betray us utterly, irrevocably. Then they, glancing at each other, smirking, will stand up, approach us, grab our suitcase and start opening it, and we, covering it with our whole body, will try to protect it from the demons, clinging to it like a kitten to its mother's nipple. We will fall to the dirty bus floor where rubbish, dirt, sand, and melted snow will smear our entire coat, our red mittens, our face, our hair. The demons will grab us by the scruff and drag us away from the suitcase. One of them will open it and discover our secret. That demon won't recognise its comrade but will be horrified, will shudder, swear, curse both the contents of the suitcase and us. The rest of the demons, loosening their grip on us, will also look into the suitcase and will also be horrified, will shudder, swear, curse both the contents of the suitcase and us. They will exchange glances and shout something to the driver, something loud and threatening, pointing out the urgent need to make an immediate stop, right in the middle of the avenue, somewhere on the side, at the kerb if possible. While one of them takes the suitcase, another one will pull out a black canvas bag from the pocket, throw it over our head, grab us by the arms and shove us out of the bus and into the frost where, on the icy surface covered with snow and sand, we together will wait under the setting sun until a patrol car comes for us and takes us to the precinct with injuries somehow still compatible with life. There in the precinct, they will drag us into the toilet, remove the bag and plunge us headfirst in yellow liquid with floating excrements. Meanwhile, they will shout at and spit on us, coercing a declaration of love to the Tsar—

Wake up. You are still on the bus. It was but a lurid dream.

We would rather not wake up. We don't know what reality we will wake up into. What if it's the wrong one?

A wrong one? What are you talking about? There has only been one to pick from, the one that you have desperately been trying to ignore. Try now.

We would rather not try anything. Trying is torture. We are but a child in a twisted lullaby.

Then wake yourself up, wake up! It cannot get worse.

It always can.

Shut up and open your

The physiognomy of the sky changes. It is tempered, not red from heat, or from blood, or as if someone up there has had an aneurysm burst, but searing white-hot, outlined with orange-red, the gradient draining somewhere beyond the horizon. The sky in all its evening grandeur laughs at you with insanity, desperation, and panic. The crimson sun, meanwhile, has almost touched the line of the horizon. It blurs and merges with its contour, and from there, from behind a veil of haze, a red sludge begins to seep out and flood the world. The sun has ceased to heat, and the air has become cosmically cold.

At last, the bus turns from the avenue onto a small one-way road, leaves behind the suburban area and enters an old, half-demolished village, where lopsided one-storey wooden houses emit vertical plumes of smoke from their brick, soot-covered chimneys. On some houses, windows are barred with rusty, crudely welded metal grilles. On others, there are shutters, some fresh, some even painted with patterns, some as old as the village, tilted or hanging on a single nail.

As the bus passes through the village, crimson dusk descends, lights are lit in the windows, and remaining people vanish from the streets. Somewhere far away, a dog barks, and somewhere nearby, a cat cries to be let in. In a minute, the village abruptly transforms into ruins. Derelict dwellings and log huts, once started and never finished, stand in the middle of wastelands and next to lone trees. The second village mirrors the first, and so then the third and the fourth. In each of them, the bus stops, discharges a few people, and moves on. The cabin empties until you are left sitting alone. The clock doesn't show 88:88 anymore, the clock is turned off. The driver yells, "Terminating here!", stops, opens the doors, and steps out to smoke, leaving the engine running.

You drag yourself onto the street, pull out the suitcase, place it on your folding trolley, look at the driver, avert your gaze, and trudge away.

The moon smoulders like an ember in the sky. The stars resemble bullet holes in a bedsheet nailed over someone's window. Sweat on your body starts to cool in the biting evening air. The steam coming out of you begins to freeze on your scarf. Shacks become sparse, no lights inside them. The ice-riddled asphalt under your feet disappears. Ahead, a bare forest looms. Its expanse is fenced with banks of old snow piled up from the road, acting as a fortress wall protecting the forest from intrusion by unwanted and uninvited guests.

Guests like us.

You step onto a trampled path, but the wheels of the trolley refuse to budge, mired in the snow like a plough in sodden spring earth. Remove the suitcase from the trolley and haul it behind you. Your body warms up and down the spine, right above the solar plexus; perspiration emerges and trickles down in small rivulets. The trees around loom taller and denser, the village light fades behind, silence and darkness envelop you like a shroud as the feeble wind stirs the tree crowns, bare and frostbitten, and rattles their branches from time to time.

We should have brought a torch.

You can't trust a torch. You should trust your instincts. Walk between the trees, the path will lead you.

But there is no path anymore.

Your face starts to tingle. Mucus oozes from your nose. You sniff. The frigid air invades, searing your nostrils, nasopharynx, and throat with icy fire. Somewhere in the distance, a dog howls. Your body fails to warm the entire cascade of sweat enveloping it. The wind doesn't just moan; it keens, echoing the distant dog's howl. Your mittened fingers gripping the suitcase handle stiffen and grow numb. The same happens in your toes, cheeks, and the tip of your nose.

Stop. Clench your fists. Open them. Repeat. Again with your toes. Rub your face vigorously with the mittens, as if to ignite it. Again, albeit fleetingly, blood starts to flow to your frost-nipped limbs. The mucus freezes in your nostrils, and when you sniff and your nose twitches, the hairs inside tense up with pain. You try to breathe through your mouth, but after a while, your lips begin to chap and sting, and the glacial air infiltrates the lungs, too.

The wind assails and retreats. The snow rises and lashes. Your body stumbles and sinks. Frozen particles of fine snow rise and lash your face like a whip, slip under your scarf and collar, and an earthbound lightning bolt of tremor courses through your body. You stumble, take a step off to the side, and, breaking the thin icy crust, your leg plunges knee-deep into a snowdrift. Your boot is now brimming with snow. Drop the suitcase and climb out. Your other leg makes a hapless step and sinks, too.

Now your boots both full of snow. Inside, it melts; the water soaks your socks, and piercing cold you feel, you shiver.

Frozen are your fingers, numb are your toes, and stiff is your resolve.

You walk. You stumble. You fall. You rise again.

We are scared.

I am scared too.

Really? Impossible.

Yes, really. More than ever.

Do you think this is the end?

Don't weep. Stop, now is not the time.

We can't, we can't. There's no better time than now.

Don't weep, lest your tears crystallise, sealing your eyes shut. There's still something to see. Feel your way along the path, any semblance of solid ground, with utmost caution. No sudden movements. Keep your feet still. First, probe for stable footing; only then, proceed, crouching to free yourself from the snow-drift's icy grip. Snow has infiltrated your sleeves and boots anew. Now shake it off, take your suitcase, survey your surroundings, and press on. Suffering beacons justice closer. Traverse the path, stand resolute. Trousers, gloves, socks—all sodden. The pulsating, ticklish warmth attempts to radiate from your heart throughout your body, gradually waning.

The trees thin, the horizon reappearing as if by magic. You quicken your pace as much as your leaden limbs allow. You drag the accursed suitcase behind, shielding your face from the sparse yet merciless gusts until you reach the precipice, colliding with a snow-blanketed bench beside a dilapidated gazebo.

Below, the frozen river valley glimmers in the moonlight. Across the chasm, atop the opposing cliff, a village flickers dimly, wisps of smoke curling from chimneys. On the horizon, a faint radiance emerges: first greenish, then azure, then violet, shimmering with gradient hues. Transfixed, mouth agape, oblivious to the wind's assault on your bleeding, frosted lips, you watch as the luminescence intensifies, expanding and drifting towards you, draping the entire sky in a colossal, undulating curtain. There, as on an obsidian altar, a fire dances, painting with light: verdant arches, cerulean spirals, and amethyst streaks akin to feathery clouds. As it nears, the cold fades from consciousness, along with your rigid limbs, the suitcase, its contents, the past days, months, seasons, years—perhaps your entire existence. When the radiance envelops you, you reach out towards the ethereal light.

It coils around your hand like a serpent, constricts, and yanks. A hoarse scream rends the air as you and the suitcase plummet down the cliff, tumbling, your mouth filling with snow. Your nostrils, eyes, every orifice in your body and clothing also clog with it until the dizzying descent ceases, the world, having turned upside down multiple times, finally comes to a halt.

You find yourself supine on the frozen river's surface. Imprinting your silhouette into the thin veneer of snow, you gaze skyward. Beside you lies the opened suitcase, its macabre contents scattered. You blink, expel the frigid water, swallow some, and gulp air greedily, wracked by coughs. Your sodden garments stiffen and harden in tandem with your numb limbs. Your crimson hat is lost, wet hair now plastered to your face. You've lost sensation in your fingers and toes as if they've ceased to exist, signalling to the rest of your body that it's time to start fading away too. Tears seep from the corners of your eyes, freezing instantly.

What now?

It seems this is the end.

What? Now?

Yes, it's about time. This is the conclusion.

We... we... what... What should we do?

... Let's make a snow angel, shall we?

II

№2: Monsters

A lurid dream there was of a cold and lightless room where inside a square fortress built under the large oak table a lonely warrior held the last outpost against the Darkness wreaking havoc upon the world. The only door in the room was locked shut. Bedsheets were nailed over the windows. Across the floor, in search of prey, snaked draught, often sneaking into the fortress, making the warrior shiver. Outside, far away, something was rumbling, something not at all like a thunderstorm.

—I'm so glad I found you, Dino. I was so scawed here alone, but together we can be brave, can't we? It's easier to be brave when you're not alone, 'specially in a fowtress like this one. Papa built it for me before he left to fight monsters and Mama said its walls were magical and they would pwotect us, but only if you and I sit here quiet. Wight. So, please, don't roar. Nobody will find us, and nobody will touch us—no monsters or evil people—because, you know, I'm scawed of monsters. They are vewy scawy, like in those horror stowies, especially those soldiers with pig faces and hooves and horns like goats have. They are vewy, vewy scawy. Super-duper scawy! I like animals, and I like piggies, but I don't like when they become monsters. The pig people have sharp tusks and make vewy scawy sounds similar to oink-oink but vewy, vewy loud and vewy, vewy harsh. Gwww! Papa used to make this kind of sound when we were play-ing, but it was not scawy because it was Papa, and he always was vewy nice, and I knew he wasn't a monster at all, so I only pwetended I was scawed when he did that. Are you scawed, Dino? I know you're not. How can you be? You're a dinosaur! Rawwwr! Wight? You have these teeth and claws and a long, heavy tail. You're vewy dangerous, but you are not a monster. I know that. You can beat any monster yourself, even the pig soldier, even if they have guns or axes, because your skin is vewy stwong, like armour or even better than armour. Actually, I think dinosaurs are scawy too, but not you, because I like you, and you're a good dinosaur. You're my fwiend, wight? Mama says I shouldn't be fwiends with scawy people, or dinosaurs, so I'm glad we can be fwiends, Dino. I was weally scawed here alone, and I cwied a little bit after Mama went out to get food, but with you, it's much better here. When she comes back, as she pwomised, you can be fwiends with her too. I have dolls, by the way, but I left them back at our home with my other toys and books and things. I would love to show them to you. I was vewy upset at first, but then I wealised that it would be vewy scawy for my dolls here because dolls fear dark castles and can't fight monsters, can they? Some of them can, but not mine. My favouwite doll's name is Mawy, by the way. She's a ballewina. I think you two could be fwiends and—

An explosion of enormous energy from afar shook the room slightly; the walls and the ceiling crackled, and the plaster dusted the fortress from above. The warrior shuddered and hugged the dinosaur.

—Mama says these are fireworks, and we should not fear them, but I don't believe her because I'm not stupid, wight? And I saw fireworks myself, and they were never loud like these bangs out there.

The warrior looked around to assure there were no spies working for Mama watching her, and whispered to the dinosaur:

—I am sure these are bombs, Dino. I saw bombs on the telly when Mama and Papa were watching a vewy loud film, and I know what sound they make.

They are vewy fun to watch on the telly, but I don't think I like when they are here. I think there should be no bombs because they are vewy scawy, and they kill people, and killing people is vewy, vewy bad. Everyone knows that. I asked Mama if we should kill monsters because monsters are also people sometimes, and she said that it is bad to kill anyone. But then I asked why Papa went killing monsters if it is bad, and then she said that Papa is pwotecting us from the monsters, and pwotecting from the monsters is good. So I couldn't decide if killing monsters is good or bad, and Mama told me that I will understand it better when I gwow up, but I think she doesn't understand that herself, even though she is vewy old and wise at her twenty-eight. All old people are sad, even when they smile, saying they are not sad. They always lie about it. My mama says she loves me even when she's sad, and I always say I love her too when I'm sad. Maybe sad people always love each other. She has become more sad when the bad things and fireworks started and Papa went to pwotect us from the monsters. She has begun saying that she loves me sometimes more than two times a day, and one day she even said that five times, and five times is a lot, vewy a lot. Do your pawents love you, Dino? I think they do. You're vewy nice. I think they are two stwong and beautiful dinosaurs, just like you, but bigger and more adult, like my pawents. We both will gwow big as our pawents are and become wise and smart and brave and maybe also a little bit sad. Do you ever feel—

Vicious pieces of metal whistled somewhere close, and the warrior leaned over, clumping her ears shut, and thus kept that position for a few minutes. When the shooting ceased, the warrior peeked from the fortress onto the window and saw that a few holes had appeared on the bedsheet covering it, with the moonlight oozing into the room. The warrior invited the dinosaur to see them.

—Don't be scawed. My mama says I should play with my imagination to scawe away the fear. You see the window? Do you know the word "constelwation"? I love this word and the things it means. I think these white dots on the bedsheet could be stars, a beautiful constelwation, maybe a dinosaur constelwation. See, they look like you, don't they? I don't know if there's a dinosaur constelwation already, but we can name this one after you. Why not? I think it's vewy gweat to have your own star, even if you can never weach it, because it is not shy, and you can still see it almost every night, and they are always there for you. Papa said they are vewy old, but I don't think they are sad, or maybe they are sad, but you can never tell they are sad. That's how bwight they are. You only see their shining and noth—

The hoof stomping rumbled in the corridor, its echo reaching the fortress and causing a floorquake. And then something let out an unearthly squeal:

—Skreeeeeee-*snort*!

The door flew off its hinges, and a bulky humanoid figure with a pig's head, clad in dark armour and armed with a gun and an axe, entered the room, its tusks smeared in blood, its horns growing from under the helmet, its odious stench rapidly replacing the air.

—Skreeeee-*snort*!—the pig soldier squealed again and began sniffing.

Inside her fortress, the warrior held her breath and embraced the silence. The pig soldier lumbered around the room, seeking prey, scraping the wooden floor with its hooves.

Another explosion thundered outside, now closer, and the whole room shook. The pig soldier spotted the table covered with a blanket, sniffed loudly, squealed, and moved towards it. There, hidden inside the fortress, the warrior kept silent, her eyes and ears closed shut. Snarling and drooling, the monster flipped the table over in one blow, throwing it aside, revealing the immobilised warrior to the Darkness, her senses still paused.

—Skreeeeeee!

Drooling and screaming, its breath smelling like a garbage bin, the pig soldier prepared to end the warrior's life. But then, from the darkness, the dinosaur, now a few metres tall, colourfully feathered creature, leapt out, roared, and plunged his sharp, white teeth right into the pig soldier's throat.

Haemorrhaging, the monster shuddered and attempted to kick the dinosaur away, but Dino strengthened his grip, clenching his jaws tighter and tighter until the soldier's neck crunched, its swollen arteries burst, and warm, dark-red blood fountained into the room.

Warm droplets spattered the warrior's face, feeling like sticky, red raindrops. The air filled with a funny smell so strong, the warrior could almost taste rusty old pennies on her tongue.

The pig soldier's last breath wheezed out and its final squeal faded into a gurgle like the last bit of bathwater going down the drain. Its head with milky-white eyes slumped down onto the floor beside his flabby, armoured body and rolled off. In the growing puddle of blood, little bubbles formed and popped, each one winking out with a tiny *bloop*. The moon-light caught the dark pool, making it shimmer like a gooey mirror.

Dead silence took over the room, and the warrior,

shaking and sobbing, opened her eyes. Her hands trembled, her fingers feeling numb and tingly. She saw the dinosaur looming over the dead pig soldier's body, his teeth covered in blood, his reptile eyes flashing in the little rays of red light coming through the holes in the bedsheet.

№3: It's Beginning to Thaw

A lurid dream there was of gaunt and ghoulish creatures wandering the frozen Earth in endless crowds of lonely souls through snow, ice, and silence. They went under the sky's eternal night, a thick and cloudy shroud above the snowy wasteland, through naked forest where wailed the northern winds, biting the creatures' faces, and where howled hungry scrawny wolves, biting the creatures' heels.

When someone froze, surrendered, fell behind, becoming one with Darkness, ravens would appear and start their morbid song. They would cover the body from above, circling and waiting until the wolves found it and tore it apart, eating the kidneys, liver, lungs, and finally, the juicy, still-beating heart. Then, once the creature's eyes lost their spark of life, the ravens would gouge them out, leaving behind empty, bloodied sockets.

The wind would drown out the scream, the blizzard would cover the tracks and remains, and the chain of creatures stretching into the distance would continue to march silently to the sound of their clattering teeth, groping for the traces disappearing under the snow right before their eyes.

In this bleak landscape, there is no trail in sight and never was, no path, only a wish to have one. To survive, one must follow a simple codex of rules that every creature knows from birth.

Creatures are born in caves, the walls of which are covered with white paintings depicting their future pilgrimage: silhouettes move towards the cave's entrance. Once a creature learns how to walk and talk, it starts learning the codex, from its parents, the magi, paintings and scrolls. It's repeated every day by everyone like a mantra and becomes memorised naturally to prepare a child for the journey. Nothing else is ever discussed, for no other topic holds relevance in the face of their impending journey. Some leave the cave as children, some as elderly, most as adults, but every day, their whole life, they study the codex.

You must walk focusing on the back in front. If there is no one in front, you go where your heart leads you. Your heart is your compass. Its pulsation accelerates when you turn the wrong way and sink into the wilderness and weakens when you slow down and start freezing.

You must light no fire. Darkness must be respected. There is nothing but it. You must not destroy the only thing you have. It means instant death, for the light attracts demons. It must be dark both outside around you and inside in your head, everywhere.

You must walk in complete silence. It must be respected, too. The world is silent for you to protect you, so must you be. Noise means instant death, for it attracts demons.

You must not think. The silence must be both in the mouth and in the head. There is no time to think because thinking heavy thoughts takes your precious energy and warmth from you. If you think, you slow down. Slowing down means instant death. You will freeze, suffer frostbite on your feet, your hands, or worse—your spirit.

You must not count steps or seconds. How long the journey takes is unknown and you must not try to change that. Don't worry about the time. In the absence of thoughts, it passes as if it does not exist. Whether an aeon or a moment, you move through unchanging lifeless emptiness, and between the beginning of the path and its end there is nothing but Darkness.

You must love Darkness. Merge with it, become its part until it reveals to you the only thing you seek.

You must always remember about Mother. Forgetting about Her means instant death. Her warm embrace awaits you at the end of your journey. Until then, it must live in the deepest caverns of your mind, guiding your heart so it could guide you.

Somewhere beyond the permafrost lands, in the mountains desperately scraping the sky with their jagged peaks, in the middle of a beautiful gorge stands Her gigantic stone statue, body bare, arms folded across Her chest, eyes closed, a lenient smile on Her face.

She was carved over millennia from a monolith by a long-forgotten tribe who knew the secret to warm life. The monolith is smooth, polished by wind and snow, and covered with symbols and patterns no one knows how to read—their language is sacred and shall forever remain unspoken and unread. The monolith extends deep, deep underground, where a holy spring boils and heats the stone, sending warmth up to the surface. There, upon touching Mother, the snow melts, and the tepid water surrounds Her and spreads in a knee-deep liquid layer around, forming a crust of ice at the circumference.

It's quiet in the gorge, peaceful. Sometimes you hear the wind. Sometimes the mountains hum as an avalanche descends elsewhere far off. Sometimes the cloudy water bubbles from the gases bursting to the surface through the cracks. Sometimes prey-seeking demons screech from above but, seeing nothing through the dense veil of vapour and gas surrounding Mother, fly away. The air carries the electrifying hint of ozone and the pungent odour of sulphur, an acrid scent that stings the nostrils and catches in the back of the throat as you enter the gorge.

Before approaching Mother, you must take off your clothes, close your eyes, put your right hand on your heart, stretch out your left hand, and walk towards the warmth. You will feel the temperature rising and your heart beating faster.

You must shiver, really shiver, not pretend—Mother recognises pretence and reserves Her blessings only for the devoted. The trembling should evenly pass through the whole body, spreading from bottom to top and penetrate every limb, corporeal and incorporeal.

Whilst you walk, your legs must not leave the water, even if you feel the water slowly corroding your skin. Keep your body above it in the biting frost. You must feel both frost and burning warmth and surrender yourself wholly to that sensation. You must walk step by step, carefully, by no means running or making sharp movements, by no means falling or creating splashes. You must not disturb the peace of Mother's dwelling.

When you reach Her incandescent feet, you must first press your lips to them, feel Her velvety skin and learn what real, enveloping, all-encompassing, all-consuming warmth is.

Only then can you put your whole body against Mother, relax, and, with Her inarticulate whisper in your ears, from the sudden heat and surge of happiness, die in bliss.

№4: Training Memory

As he listened to the lulling clank of a train, Gwyg sat next to his father and gazed at his homeland retreating into the distance, a village nestled among the balding knolls, the same knolls where he had witnessed his birth and boyhood.

Somewhere beyond those hills was their home, from which he felt he had not yet journeyed that far away, at least not by rail; on foot, he thought, they had certainly walked quite a distance. Somewhere there was also the blooming apple orchard, which after last year's break should burst into maroon glory again. Ripe and heavy with juice, apples would tumble to the green grass, laden and tired of hanging and wishing to be picked, then baked into a fragrant cinnamon apple pie, pressed into juice, mashed into purée, boiled into jam or compote, or simply eaten, perhaps after removing wee worms and slicing off the rusty brownish spots, which Gwyg had deemed as a child to be the tastiest parts. Somewhere there also lay a field where they had just planted potatoes, which this year, presumably, his mother and sister would dig out alone. There was also the white building of a school he had just graduated from, and each labyrinthine passageway and pedagogical chamber was etched with impeccable clarity in his memory. Some of his friends were still there, but some jounced on this same train, chattering like an audience in a theatre that didn't quite understand the play's plot. Still there were also his favourite teachers, from whom he had parted amidst a bittersweet farewell a few weeks ago together with his classmates and Ann.

His mind was wracked with poignant remorse, a melancholic afterthought that nagged at him relentlessly, for not being able to say goodbye to Ann in person, resorting instead to a phone. Gwyg hated phones; they seemed unnatural to him, a lifeless medium of communication bereft of warmth and tactility. It filled him with unspoken anxiety that the phone might become the only way to keep in touch with his home and kin. Gwyg was sure the invention of the telephone was a callous ploy to delude people into thinking that they no longer needed face-to-face interactions and could simulate communication via a hissing relay travelling electrical conduits. Hearing a cherished voice transmitted across vast distances did stir a delight, yes, yet it always remained a pale imitation of the genuine, an ersatz approximation. His hatred of phones intensified even more because he had to listen to Ann's distorted dulcet voice at the moments when he yearned to lose himself in the sky-like boundless depth of her eyes and see the reflections of drifting clouds, to hug her, run his fingers through her silken hair, and just stand like that for a few minutes without separating, feeling her eyelashes tickling his cheek.

As the landscape blurred by, chugging along the rails, emotions and feelings came and went, amalgamated, and clogged his train of thought. Abruptly, Gwyg felt a wrenching nostalgia, which he had never felt before, vivid and luminous, as if memories, like Gwyg, his father, and others on the train now, were being transferred to another part of the brain, to a cerebral factory where they underwent a metamorphosis by a complex alchemical interplay into nostalgic material for subsequent revision. Somehow, Gwyg felt that part of these memories would remain just memories caught in the same temporal trap as the present moment.

A chilling sensation slithered up his spine to his neck, and felt like the quivers of an impending shiver, yet halted midway in its ascent. Gradually, Gwyg began to feel uneasy, like a taut rope stretched thin by the force of distance. He sensed that a piece of himself had been taken away from him, that his body was still there, but a part of him, be it his soul or the proverbial consciousness or something else metaphysical, was still at home with his mother and sister, drinking tea, relishing the crumbly texture of oatmeal cookies studded with tart cranberries, which his mother had baked early in the morning. She must have got up at five or six o'clock for this, or maybe she hadn't slept all night. That morning, she appeared fatigued and somewhat disoriented, her eyes reddened as if she had been cutting onions all night, and she seemed to have aged a few years. Gwyg even thought he saw some grey hair on her head.

A sudden realisation struck Gwyg that if they were to meet next time, they would all be completely different people, and his sister would have grown up and become a big adult girl, and he, Gwyg, would miss that transformation. She would always stay that mischievous monkey whom he, just a few minutes ago, could pick up with both hands and lift skyward, spin around on a laughing carousel, or put her astride his shoulders and run along the river's edge.

Gwyg's father, also dressed in khaki, sat next to him the whole time and remained silent. Perhaps he had no words left to be spoken, or that part that had been cleaved from everyone on that day and taken away was too agonising to bear. He didn't look sad, tired, or upset—he looked none, thought Gwyg, with empty eyes and a face devoid of emotion as though he were a machine, shut off and left to gather dust. He was never an emotional person; it was difficult to call him sentimental or sensitive to anything. Rather, he reacted stoically, using frowning, headshaking, or expressing passive disapproval with his calm demeanour, but now it was as if he had put on a mask. It was still his face, but someone else was hiding behind its guise. Gwyg couldn't know what was going on in his father's head, whether he was thinking about home or whithersoever they were going and what would happen next. Perhaps his father was thinking about the same things, the same people, his wife and daughter, trying to memorise their faces with forced smiles as they stood on the platform among a hundred others and remember them like this, without tears in their eyes, although with a touch of sadness that would never be washed out of his memory whatever happens.

Gwyg never thought that his first train ride with his father would be like this. Soon they were supposed to go to the city, to the university, where his father, dressed in his best suit, which, as Gwyg's mother said, he had kept since the wedding and was now slightly tight on his belly, would lead Gwyg to the table of the admission office in the polytechnic faculty. After presenting Gwyg's pile of papers and school diploma with his decent but average scores, he would say that his son wanted to become an engineer. The admission office member would smile, they would hand over all the necessary documents, and the two would go to have their first beer together. Then in the evening, Gwyg would finally meet Ann again.

The horizon's voracious maw devoured their home. At first, hand-waving people turned into small smeared silhouettes, then cars disappeared, then trees and houses melded into a uniform grey-green goop before dissolving entirely, and finally, the church's spire dove beyond the horizon and the village faded away. Amidst the fading landscape, a scraggly and scruffy stray, with a torn ear and a possible limp, chased after them, but then it stopped in the middle of the rails and just continued barking at the passing train until it too merged with the landscape. Later, as they descended into a valley, a river began to run by the side, the same one where Gwyg once learned to swim, and where he went fishing with his father or friends, but then the river sharply turned and the train entered an endless pine tunnel, which, due to the movement, looked more like a poorly assembled shoddy stockade, reminiscent of the ones their ancestors built to protect their settlements.

The wind wafted the scent of resin and pine needles into the coach through an ajar window. The monotonous panorama of pines and the clattering of the train's wheels soothed and entranced Gwyg. As his thoughts began to drift away and ennui crept in, he feared he would succumb to sleep and miss the whole journey leaving no memory of it behind so he decided to talk.

—Which front exactly are they taking us to?— Gwyg asked.

His father turned his face to him and only shrugged.

№5: Fluffislav The Fearsome

Should there exist any risk or a hint of danger, it was worth the pleading eyes of Fluffislav Fluffinsky. Thus thought Lena, returning home through the musty and damp corridors of the forsaken manufactory, half of which, she knew, even though it happened years before she even saw the light, was subjected to bombardment during the Great Coup and was never restored nor demolished, but instead turned into a locale of interest, an amusement park for people with an abundance of leisure hours, including children like herself or older, rarely younger, persons with no fixed abode, persons who were "into substances", and other, rather shady and "unbelievably dangerous", types, as Lena's dear mother, Mrs Zakonnik, warned her, trying to dissuade her in any possible way from going to the manufactory.

She did not think much about her decision or its consequences when picking up a cat, and not just a cat, a black cat—it was an instinctive, impulsive, irresistible action, and many other in-s, im-s and ir-s, for encountering a cat ("Kitten!") at that time was akin to encountering a unicorn, an animal, for the record, of equal thaumaturgic potency, albeit, in the case of a cat, a thaumaturgy ominous and sly. It wasn't Lena's opinion—hardly did she have any opinion on cats beyond pure childish curiosity—it was the Tsar's, therefore everyone's. Cats, he was rumoured to have said, are evil omens, enemies of the state, hence they have no place in the utopia, especially black cats, which undoubtedly are devilish entities, and should be banned, subjected to felicide and never again seen in Novo Tsarstvo. Nobody knew the inward reasons behind that decision and could only speculate whether their leader was simply a superstitious individual who saw black cats as harbingers of misfortune and decided to eliminate the potential source of bad luck by stigmatising all the cats, even the ones of other colours, for even they, with a certain chance, could give birth to a little black demon that would later wreak havoc on the state of utopia; whether ailurophobia could be one of the flaws of their fearless leader; whether it was a childhood trauma and the scar on the Tsar's cheek was, in fact, left by a black cat;

whether it was a prophecy woven into the Tsar's mind by his personal seer that predicted the Tsar's downfall linked to a black cat; or whether a cat was a symbol of rebellion, freedom, pure anarchy, too unpredictable and independent, too slothful and therefore failing to contribute sufficient amounts of value to the utopian economy.

All that could hardly bother Lena, for not only was she young and eager to break the rules for the sake of breaking the rules and keen to explore for the sake of adventure, but also because before meeting Fluffislav she had seen a cat once in a picture in a book that she too found at the same manufactory and could only dream of them yet remaining somewhat uncertain that the creature she saw and was now carrying home was indeed a cat, shaggy, with tangled fur, with a scruffy ear and a bald tail in two places. "Perhaps, it's a weird furry rat and I'm just being silly," she thought, but she knew what rats looked like. "Perhaps, it's an otter," she thought, but their appearance was even more obscure to her than that of cats, and moreover, what would an otter be doing at the abandoned manufactory in the Town T? "That would've been even sillier, you silly young lady." Therefore, the cat being a cat was self-evident, and the name "Fluffislav Fluffinsky", or "Fluffislav" for short, was self-evident too and occurred to her inexorably, immediately, irrevocably (and other adverbs Lena had learned recently and liked to use, and which, in their feline-like daring nature, too were stigmatised by some), for the kitten was, well, quite fluffy.

—Whatever it takes, you're with me now, Fluff-islav,—she patted the cat and hid him under her jacket close to her heart.—We're in this together.

—Miaouw,—responded Fluffislav, and this very "miaouw" and the purr that accompanied it were, indeed, worth the risk, too.

—Whatever it takes,— she added, goosebumped all over.

Lena walked alerted through deserted promenades, barren tracts, rubbish heaps, encountering other abandoned objects, some of which included those very people of no fixed abode whom she, by the way, knew by name, and who, in fact, were intelligent and interesting people despite everything her dear mother had told her, through quiet, unpeopled and rubbish-strewn streets, and streets peopled but still quiet and still strewn with rubbish, filled with silent grey figures with sour faces that headed somewhere, perhaps, she thought, to do their important work for the state. She approached her home, a nine-storey grey panel building, greeted the old ladies who gathered at the entrance and conversed about quotidian matters that were none of their business ("senile witches", as Lena called them in return to them claiming her "a little imp, not a girl" for reasons she wouldn't disclose), summoned the lift, a small metal cabin turned into a canvas, a place of artistic expression of someone whose name she wouldn't disclose either, travelled to her sixth floor, and finally entered her flat, where her dear mother, as she always did when at home, nervously awaited her daughter's return.

—What's that?— a mask of eldritch horror crept over Mrs Zakonnik's face.

—Fluffislav,— Lena answered with an expression of complete and total normality as if Fluffislav was, in fact, her brother whom she had picked up from a nursery.

—Fluffi-what?

—Fluffislav Fluffinsky. I think he's a cat.

Mrs Zakonnik's eyes and lips opened wide, she clutched her head and began pacing around the room, muttering to herself some incantations as if she, sometimes also called a senile witch by her daughter, had really become one, doing it in the same way Lena's crazy old uncle, her mother's dear brother, acted a few days before he was sent away to an institution specialising in treating such odd behaviour, so Lena naturally grew worried.

—What's wrong?

Discombobulated, Mrs Zakonnik shook her head ("Tsar help me!"), and kept shaking it throughout the rest of the conversation.

—Go... go... go into your room, Lena.

—But Mum—

—Don't argue with your mother!

—But Mum—

—I said go into your room, young lady.

Mrs Zakonnik was terrified and, well, furious, at the same time, both of which, in addition to her appearance at that moment and her appearance in general, including her aquiline facial features, did indeed make her resemble a witch ("Senile witch!").

—And this...—she pointed at the cat with her finger, now jerking like a jackhammer.—"Thing"... Throw it out of the window.

—What?

—I said get rid of this "thing".

—It's not a "thing", Mum.

Lena didn't like the tone of the conversation, and the sound of the "thing", and the connotations it implied in particular, made her rather disturbed and angry, too.

—Then I'm going to do it myself,—she said, reaching her hand towards Fluffislav.—Give it to me. Now.

—I'm not giving him to you.—Lena said, stepping back.

—I will flush this "thing" (!) down the toilet.

—Miaouw,—Fluffislav felt like he must contribute to the discussion.

In response, Mrs Zakonnik squealed, hopping and slamming her hand against the door jamb.

—I hoped it was dead already at least! Lena! Do you want to kill your mother?

—Maybe I do! If you harm Fluffislav!— shouted Lena and, holding Fluffislav in her arms, retreated to her room and locked herself there, leaving her mother petrified and speechless.

—You know it's against the law, silly young lady? Do you want to go to prison at your age? What would our neighbours think? Antitsarism!—grumbled Mrs Zakonnik through the key hole.

But no answer followed. Knowing the protocols as any state servant must, Mrs Zakonnik hurried to take the phone ("Tsar help me!"), in the process entangling herself in the wire, and started spinning the rotary dial, failed a few times, but, in the end, after a dozen attempts, reached the Local Bureau of Comprehensive Documentation, Information Management, Archival Integrity, and Data Compilation Services, LBCDIMAIDCS for short, the place where she, as a valuable citizen awarded multiple times with "the employee of the year" badge, had been proud to work since the age of twenty, and heard the bored voice of her friend on the other side of the wire. During their brief and fussy conversation, she didn't mention the "thing" and, moreover, she tried with her voice and words to pretend that nothing of such scale had happened at all, and she just needed, for some reason she couldn't disclose, an inspection at her home to discuss some legal matters and concerns over the events compromising national security she encountered recently in the city that certainly and strictly were NOT related to her daughter. Her bored friend, Mrs Coupoff, a woman of ample proportions, ample soul and no less ample inquisitiveness, now devoid of her unremitting ennui and excited about the veritable affair of Mrs Zakonnik's phone call, knew whom to call next and happily did so. Thereafter the request echoed through the city electrically in a chain of consecutive phone calls, a friend calling a friend, an acquaintance calling an acquaintance, nephews and nieces calling their aunts and uncles, lost some and acquired new enigmatic details along its journey, and, from a hectic request for legal advice, transformed into somewhat of a code-red, and summoned a local state inspector.

That gentleman, who was called Mr Ailuroff, clad in black clothes, and wearing a black fedora hat, which all contrasted vividly with his sickly white skin, having the look of a man of the utmost importance and impeccable state secrecy because of the afore-mentioned outfit and his demeanour, upon packing his fears and genuine interest regarding the matter, jumped into his black luxury car, put a blinker on the roof, and headed to Zakonniks', where Mrs Zakonnik, who had already managed to brush up a little and calm down, met Mr Ailuroff at the door and with fastidious bureaucratic conduct and indifference explained to him the true nature of the occasion. The inspector, honestly, couldn't believe his ears, for such an event, an event involving, Tsar forbid, a cat, was considered rare, nay impossible, and often was associated with phone terrorism, such as when someone called from a telephone booth on the street and said that there was a cat in the building, for instance, in a theatre showing a quite dissident performance, and now it must be urgently evacuated to eradicate the devilish entity and keep the citizens safe, thereby the inspector had doubts. Mrs Zakonnik, nevertheless, convinced Mr Ailuroff that the matter was indeed important and the cat indeed existed, and he, now slightly anxious and even more sickly white, decided to check the evidence before retiring back. With his gloved fist, the inspector knocked at Lena's door.

—Young lady, hello, I am Mr Ailuroff.

—I'm Lena, Mr Geezer.

—Lena, tell me, have you really found "a cat"?

—I think so.

—You think so? So you're not sure?

—I don't know. I think I am.

—Is it still with you?

—He is.

Mr Ailuroff, who himself had never seen a real cat, gulped and retreated a pace back from the door as fear and thrill intermingled in his stomach, then looked at Mrs Zakonnik and gestured to her something she couldn't understand and only shrugged in response.

—Do you know it's illegal to keep a cat?

—My dear mother has kindly informed me, yes.

—Then don't you want to dispose of the creature?

—He's not "a creature" or "a thing". His name is Fluffislav Fluffinsky. I want you to refer to him by his name. And I'm not going to "dispose" of him. He now is my friend, Mr Geezer. You can go away.

—This is not how the protocol works, young lady.

—Helena.

—Helena, miss, this is not how it works. We should bag your Fluffislav and deliver it to the analysis and disposal service.

—You should bag yourself and fuck off.

—Helena!—exclaimed Mrs Zakonnik as the inspector threw her a glance full of brooding discontent.—I apologise, inspector, my girl doesn't understand what she's saying. She's just a child.

—No, I'm not!

Mr Ailuroff nodded to Mrs Zakonnik, and continued:

—What colour is the creature?

—He's not a creature. His name is Fluffislav, I told you already. And he's black.

A frisson of terror went through Mr Ailuroff's body, from his very toes to his very top, as he emitted a sound resembling a stifled shriek of a person being poured over with ice-cold water ("This cannot be, can it?") The inspector swallowed a massive lump again.

—Are you sure... it is black?

—Black as the night. I can show you.

—Wait, please stay in the room. I... I believe you.

—Are you sure, inspector?

—I am quite sure... We don't yet truly know... what kind of dangers to the national security this particular... "sample" may possess.

At this point, a latch clicked, Mr Ailuroff leaned backwards, but found himself against Mrs Zakonnik's breasts ("Pervert!") and then met her terrified eyes. The door opened, and from there appeared Lena hugging Fluffislav, who, unlike his previous appearance, looked cuddly and even fluffier, for Lena, while her dear mother was busy telephoning and then recovering and before the inspector arrived, had brushed the cat and given him milk.

—I want to show Fluffislav to you. Here, look how cute and harmless he is,—Lena said and, holding Fluffislav in both hands, pulled them forward, presenting the stretched-out cat to the audience in all his feline beauty. From his mouth, a little pink tongue peeked playfully, and his eyes, agape, gleamed verdantly like diluted tarragon lemonade, as deep as the voidest void. Fluffislav's vertical pupils dilated horizontally, and he uttered:

—Miaouw.

A demonic yell erupted from Mr Ailuroff's mouth as, startled, he shuddered, hopped and dropped his carpetbag, while Mrs Zakonnik, upon experiencing the very same emotion, clawed at the inspector's coat and hid behind his back. As a prompt reaction to such an insolent, impolite, irreverent act, Fluffislav, fright-ened himself, leaped out from Lena's hands onto the floor and hissed, which, in turn, imposed even more horror on Mr Ailuroff and he, without a second thought (the first thought was "Tsar have mercy!"), as if it were his primordial instinct, took his fedora off and threw it at Fluffislav, which, hurled with masterful skill, covered little Fluffislav as a dome. Stunned, Lena could not even fathom what was going on, for it was unfolding with such prodigious celerity that it felt like a single moment, and later, as soon as she saw cupolaed Fluffislav and reached her hands towards him, the cat, not able to get rid of the hat, started racing across the room in wild panic, and, after a few hasty circles around Mr Ailuroff and Mrs Zakonnik, assailed them. Well, for them, in their current condition, it seemed like an act of savage brutality, whilst Fluffislav, bereft of his sight, only attempted to liberate himself by jumping in a random direction. Mr Ailuroff let forth a shrill cry, convulsively grabbed his carpetbag and dashed away towards the front door. At the same time, Lena uplifted the frightened kitten and cradled him to her chest ("Dumb adults...").

—Dispose of it!—shouted Mr Ailuroff through his clenched teeth, looking at the hosts, and, arming himself with his index finger, gestured floorward.—I wasn't here! Bedlam!—the inspector added, either indicating the state of the affairs in the room or hinting at his next destination, ran away and no soul has seen him since.

№6: Dream

Every time in my lurid dream, I shoot, but he refuses to die, the bastard. My heart stops as I cock the hammer and hold my breath, then slowly, as if squeezing a succulent fruit, I pull the trigger. The same flash at the barrel's end, the same sharp bang echoing into the distance and buzzing in my ears, the same narcotic sulphurous smell, the same numbness in my shoulder. I transform into a bullet and fly, liberated, as if my body no longer matters or exists—I'm a saviour, I'm a goddess of death. I savour every sensation when I enter his skull, slicing through his thin, wrinkled skin, grinding his bone like a fake piece of porcelain, digging deep into his brain—I'm in the most abominable place in the world, slimy and sly, empty of love and full of shit. His dying convolutions suffocate me, his merciless thoughts plead for mercy running behind me, but I exit his head out on the other side, leaving behind a trail of blood and brain bits. The Tsar falls to the ground, silently, as the crowd around him gasps in a mix of awe, fear and relief, all at the same time and none to the fullest. Here, my life as a bullet ends, again and again and again. But every time, as soon as I realise the bastard is still alive for one reason or another, I jump up from my bunk in a feverish sweat that pours off me, soaking the sheets.

I'm in my childhood room in my father's flat. My skin shrivels as I step on ice-cold discoloured linoleum, sending a shiver back and forth through my pale body. I approach the window, open the curtains, sit on the windowsill naked and start smoking out of the vent. The sun reflects off the snow and mirrors right into my eyes. The papirosa smoke refuses to crawl out onto the street and just swirls around me. On the bare black tree dusted with snow, bullfinches have settled at oddly regular intervals, red like plump apples.

I hate them fucking bullfinches. Yesterday, after I came here, I took down their wooden birdhouse from the tree and smashed it against the pavement, yet they keep flying here, perching on the black branches and staring at me.

I remember the crunch of snow as I dragged along with my father through the city outskirts, trying not to step on protruding rebars and not fall through an open manhole. He was carrying an air rifle on his back and a papirosa in his teeth. I was carrying a bag of tin men, figurines we had cut out of his beer cans together. I made fun of how the stars from the beer logo miraculously ended up where the hearts of these men were supposed to be. My father walked confidently in front of me, paving the way, whilst I staggered along, trying to find his footprints with my little frozen feet. If I were to say I was freezing, he would've led me right back home. I didn't want that, I wanted to shoot. It was frosty, but the cold was pleasant, tickled rather than bit, reddened my cheeks. It was bright; I had to squint, just like now. I've always loved days like this. It's that kind of day that reminds you that you love winter nonetheless.

We came to a desolate yard of an abandoned manufactory. My father trusted me to hold the rifle whilst he took the bag from me and went to remnants of the foundation of a demolished building to arrange the figurines, carefully putting them at oddly regular intervals. The targets were a few metres away but in my memory they were right in front of my face, as far away as the fucking bullfinches are now.

—Remember, baby girl, shooting is not just about pulling a trigger,—my father told me, and I believed him. Discipline, patience, posture, grip, breathing—of course, these are also important, but as soon as your finger hits the trigger different things start to matter. He offered to let me shoot first, took the rifle in his hands, pressed its butt against my shoulder, pre-padding it with his knitted cap. The figurines were already on the scope; there were seven of them, a lucky number. I chose the second one from the end. I don't know why. It seemed to me, silly girl, the chances to miss were lower, for it looked more miser-able than the others. My father hugged me from behind, helped me point the rifle, reminded me to close my other eye. I nodded, swallowed, stilled. Impatient, all I could think of was how in a second my father would shout "well done" and we would go together to see where the figurine had fallen. And lo and behold, in the middle of the shimmering blinding snowdrifts, I saw a star in the scope, but the moment I squeezed my index finger, out of nowhere, right in front of the tiny tinny man, a fucking bullfinch appeared, red as a plump apple, and a second later they both fell into the snow together. I remember him lying there on the white glistening snow with his grey wings spread, making a snow angel. I didn't know whether to worry and cry because I had killed the poor bird or to rejoice at my remarkable marks-manship.

A lurid dream there was, a week ago or so, a

bullfinch was sitting on the Tsar's head, and I, hidden on the roof, was watching them through the scope. It felt theatrical: people were emerging and disappearing but I couldn't see their faces, automobiles were passing with no fume, the wind was singing but I didn't feel it. It was the only time I knew for sure it was a dream, my fantasy, and not just another day at work, because of that bird. Magically undetected, the bullfinch had landed on the Tsar's head when the motorcade stopped and he got out of the car, surrounded by two muscular louts. On the rooftop on the other side of the square sat my colleague, and possibly several others who had not been reported to me.

As usual, I watched the bastard walk, raising his hand feebly to wave to the crowd of civil servants forced to be there, struggling to put on smiles or at least neutral expressions instead of their gargoyle faces. If one of these angry and sullen faces suddenly jumped out of the crowd armed with a shiv or an awl, I should have shot the poor fellow. He would fall, the louts would grab the Tsar under his arms and drag him back to his armoured car. The crowd, meanwhile, would freeze like mannequins, and their jaws would clench like those of a nutcracker. The sound of that would fill the air and make it vibrate, creating odd optical illusions, similar to what you see in a hot desert. The family and friends of the culprit would be found, interrogated meticulously, the rest of the conspirators would be identified, and they all together would be put against the wall at oddly regular intervals and taught love for the Tsar. In my memory that happened only once, when the Tsar was ostentatiously buying ice-cream from a fake saleswoman. Suddenly a bloke from the crowd rushed at him from behind, shouting, but after my shot, collapsed on his ruler, covering him. After that the security measures swelled to paranoid proportions; the Tsar was not seen in public for several months. But then, apparently to prove that he was still alive, he came out to people again. That time only on the stage, as he put it, away from the scum.

Distracted again. The dream.

So, lo and behold, with the fucking bullfinch on his head the bastard walks, barely moving his legs, as if he had porridge instead of kneecaps. The bird flutters on his bald head, nesting, asking for a bullet. I feel like it's smirking at me as much as a bird could do. I can see that from the scope. The bird whispers something unrecognisable. It is where I should aim, slightly higher than the bastard's head.

But I know my objective.

In my dream, I'm always that poor fellow-traitor, sitting on the roof with a weathered face and dry, cracked lips. The Tsar appears in front of the tribune and as he opens his mouth I pull the trigger with orgasmic pleasure. At this point, everything except the bastard, the bird, and the bullet disappears, as if someone has cleared the stage—it's a grey-blue emptiness, in which the target is about to meet his portion of lead. He falls before he can utter a word. The bullfinch flaps its wings and flies away. My heart beats arrhythmically, like a shaman's drum. A victory, finally, a glorious victory. I've saved them, the crowd of nutcrackers.

The next moment, I find myself, already beaten, in a torture room. It's just me, a flickering light bulb, and the interrogator, an old man with an utterly mental smile, deranged slanted eyes and an ugly hussar moustache, wearing a white coat and disproportional black rubber gloves. I hear how he giggles connecting electrodes to my head. The room, at the same time, begins shrinking into itself slowly, walls and ceiling moving towards me with a jittering motion. The interrogator says in a funny voice, "Girl, baby girl, it was just a double. What did you think?" My eyes widen. I taste iron in my mouth. I've bitten my tongue, bitten it off. With an angry snort, I roll a piece of it in my mouth, giving my palate a last chance to feel what it's like to be me, to feel the taste of myself before I spit it in his face. In response, he laughs at me and pulls a knob. The electric current flows through the wires into my brain like an avalanche and I smell my smoked skin, the scent no different from a smoked, freshly killed hog. The room shrinks into itself further. Nothing. The end of it.

You know those little bittersweet memories from childhood which, upon stumbling upon in adulthood, stir something inside? For someone it's a smoked hog or the taste of iron on your lips; for others it may be the smell of seaberry, or rather seaberry kissel, that jelly thing my grandmother brewed every time I came to visit her for the summer; or the smell of freshly cut grass, which we mowed together with my father in the evenings; or the taste of my mother's pastries with that special spice. Sometimes it seems that you have forgotten that little memory, perhaps for years, a lacuna in your personal history, but then suddenly it finds you in the crowd, slaps you on the shoulder, says your name, in a voice still so strange, seemingly filled with familiar yet alien notes. You turn around, and it asks, "Is that you? Do you recognise me?" You're all confused, standing there, befuddled and lost, unable to figure out who that is standing in front of you with the arms outstretched, smiling full thirty-two. Only after a few seconds you understand everything, and in your head, having risen from the bottom, casting off the mud, blooms a flower of memories. It can be ugly or beautiful or sometimes both.

For me, the main such detail was not the bullfinches, not any of the things I mentioned before, but the melodic clanking of my father's typewriter. It was impossible to hide from it in our flat. He would start in the morning, continue all day long with short breaks for bitter coffee and a papirosa on the balcony and end at night in the kitchen where my mother would send the late typist, pointing out that he was "clattering like a broken locomotive". In response, he would shrug, kiss her on her forehead and, hugging his typewriter, leave their room for the kitchen, where the balcony was nearer for smoking purposes, and a bin for failed manuscripts was ready to be overflown so that a mountain of crumpled sheets of paper would appear there in the morning. I was used to that rhythmic clanking from infancy. It was natural to me, as natural as the ticking of a clock or the noise from a telly. Sometimes it even lulled me to sleep, calmed me down and helped me to concentrate. I listened to it not only at home but also at my father's workplace.

After school, on my way back, I often went to his papirosa-scented office, where he would sit with his back tense and almost straight and type something, moving his fingers with great speed, never seeming to miss the keys. But if he really didn't miss them, where would the mountains of crumpled drafts come from, I wonder? He would sit me down next to him, put a book in my hand, and I would wait for him to finish his important journalistic work so that we could go home together. On our way through the snowy narrow streets lazily illuminated with lamp lanterns he would complain to me about how the world was heading decadenceward, and our country, already Novo Tsarstvo at that time, with it—if not like a locomotive, at least like a draisine, on which, he said, we were jumping up and down, up and down, with utter lack of enthusiasm.

Sometimes, when he was busy, I would sit with him until late into the evening, and whilst listening to the clanking, I would lazily leaf through my textbook and try to squeeze out my maths homework. His office was small: one desk, two towering bookcases, one metal filing cabinet, three ashtrays, a tea-blackened mug, an old pre-Coup poster with the Colossus still standing sentinel over the city, and one plant with yellowed leaves in the corner. He didn't even have a proper window; it was more of a cubbyhole than a room. He smoked right there, smoked a lot, so we were both sitting in an odorous cloud. I liked the scent; I still do, not as much as the taste—it's rather disgusting—but the scent reminds me of him. His colleagues would come to see him, they would smoke together, laugh, and discuss things I didn't understand, like the historical role of our nation in the fate of the world or the ambiguity of the political situation in the country. They thought the changes the country was going through, the reestablished Tsarism, the commencing censorship, all were just colourful balloons sent into the air to distract the masses and give them things to talk about and didn't have "any substance", for no true change is possible in our country, yet arguing about it all seemed necessary.

After those talks, we would come home in the dark and barge into the flat, covering the threshold with melting snow from our wet boots, coats and hats. Our mother would meet us there, not angry or upset, just tired of waiting for us. At that time the tragedy had yet to befall us, she was still alive, my father was completely different, the country was different, my whole world was different, everything was much simpler and clearer, and I had not yet learnt how to shoot.

I remember how once I went to his workplace; the building was abuzz; his colleagues ran around in chaos through the corridors like bees in a disturbed hive, flying in and out of their cells, passing something to each other, whilst some sat on the floor, pulling their hair. I walked down the corridor to his office on the third floor. His door was open, and then my father himself, frowning and hunched over, came out hugging a large grey-brown box full of manuscripts, books, folded posters, ashtrays, that tea-blackened mug and other work supplies. He set the box on the floor next to the door, reached for the plaque with his name and job title mounted on the wall, took it off and looked at it for a while, tossed it carelessly into the box, and, finally noticing me, stretched out a nervous half smile. He was, as he had told my mother at the time, one of many "relieved of their duties," whether for the words they had printed or because of the place they all worked in—it didn't matter nor does it now. He was not hired for another job. "Higher authorities," as he thought, had sent letters to all the other magazines, newspapers, and publishers, and wherever he went, whether his friends were there or not, all they could say was, "Sorry, we can't do anything, it's a decree from above. Period." All he could find was a night-time hustle as a watchman at the local library where they let him put a typewriter in, so he kept writing whilst "working". Every day he brought home a few pages, their number dwindling over time until it reached nil. He always considered himself a true patriot who wanted to love his motherland with open eyes, but it always resisted such love in every possible way. In that situation, you either stop loving or close your eyes. My father seemed to have chosen the latter, retreating into a patriotic dreamworld.

All I regret now, and probably will regret as long as I live, is that I missed his transformation from a slender, energetic and handsome young man to a hunched, shrivelled, skinny, scraggly fifty-year-old geezer; how he went from the one who taught me about life, morality, ethics, arts, to the one who didn't even turn a deaf ear when his daughter took and threw away the birdhouse, and now observes them bullfinches left without a home, smoking the hell knows which papirosa; how he went from someone who spent nights typing daring notes for his political column to someone who spent nights drunk, surrounded by empty nips and cans with those same star logos, sitting and staring with cloudy eyes at the telly with a shimmering stream of idiocies on the screen. They confabulated the past, rewrote it, almost, as if no atrocities ever existed—only glorious victories. They spread conspiracy theories about biological weapons, the red sludge turning you into a demon. They simulated a nuclear strike on our neighbours and showed it on Channel One in prime time. They perverted the language, and objects and concepts, both ugly and beautiful, swapped their meanings. They broadcasted a leaderboard of the number of people our delusional soldiers killed during the invasion. They said we're victims and don't have a choice but to protect ourselves. The snow angel, originally rhyming with a dove of peace, was banned, by irony, as an extremist symbol. And they did all of it in such a subtle and persuasive manner that somehow my father believed it. I cannot imagine what they would've been able to achieve if they only were more competent.

When we were left alone with him, we stopped talking and only checked up on how each other was doing, the proverbial things, weather and health. It was like there was nothing to talk about anymore. Talking had become scary. I wanted to comfort him but nobody taught me how to do that. I was angry with him for it because HE was an adult and HE knew his way with words, not me, so he should've said something, at least a sentence or two. I was angry as if everyone else is taught to talk about dead relatives but he didn't want to pass this knowledge on to me. From one social nucleus, we divided and retreated into our separate bubbles. It soon became unbearable to throw out his empty bottles, to wash his vomit off the carpets, to clean the flat, to cook, to sleep over at my friends' half of the time. I didn't want any of that, I was sixteen.

You know that the easiest way to offend an alcoholic, a real alcoholic, is to tell him that he is drunk even though he is sober at that moment. His normal state of mind is lost and it becomes difficult to say what causes this or that behaviour—whether it's alcohol or the fact that he has been so soaked in it that his old personality has dissolved or evaporated. My father was always genuinely offended when I taunted, asking if he was drunk again despite all his futile efforts not to drink. Yes, at one point I thought he was still trying. Who knows, maybe it was after I asked him this question again that he got angry at me, at himself, at any attempts to quit, and went back to boozing. And so, if I saw him in a state even remotely resembling sobriety, I tried not to question it, not to talk to him. I was supposed to be glad that he was trying and appreciate his attempts. Shouldn't I have been? But one day, after listening to another "lecture" from him, a short extract on how I was full of hatred and spite towards my own country and thus to him, for the first time I caught myself thinking that I wasn't happy about his sobriety at all, and I left. Any fast-spinning thought that what my father was saying might be his true thought and not part of a distorted mind was terrifying. It was devastating to realise that it wasn't his delusions that were delirious but the order of things.

"Dream on, girl, dream big," he'd told me a long time ago. But no matter how hard I tried, I couldn't think of anything to dream about except for the end of it all as soon as possible in any way imaginable. Yeah, that way too. Loving someone and wishing them dead at the same time is excruciatingly hard and would probably destroy me, yet it seemed to me that for the nightmare to end and for things to get back to normal, someone had to die, someone containing a lump of negative energy so heavy that it was anchoring my world to the bottom. I quickly decided who it had to be besides my father and me, and the thought, nasty, viscous as a slimy sly slug, snuck into my head, leaving a stinking trail on my body, entering through my ear, through my mouth, or through one of my nostrils—any of those orifices, or was born right there from a maggot that everyone has planted in their heads from birth. I'm sorry, I don't know how those thick, ugly creatures with teeth like a spiked-inside collar are born, but I can feel them there in my head, crawling between the folds of my brain, eating me from the inside, showing me those same lurid dreams.

I shouldn't have given my emotions a chance to compromise my mission, but recently, years since I left, I decided to visit him right before this final day. I'm a different person now, with a different name, for whom he is a nobody, not even a part of the past. I didn't know if he would recognise me, or if I would recognise him, and to be honest, I expected that no one would open the door for me and I would have to knock on the neighbours' doors to learn he was dead. But when I got to our tower block, I found him lying face down in a drift with his hands drowned in the snow. I knew it was him at once. I pulled the drunken man out of the drift and dragged him into our old flat. It was minus twenty-five and his hands were blue, covered in frost, seemingly icy, too fragile, almost about to shatter like a crystal glass. Luckily, he hadn't lost his keys.

The house smelt of smoke, as usual. The heavy dark-brown curtains were shut; only a single ray of sunlight was oozing inside. I felt like I had entered a musty dungeon or a big coffin, a tomb that pharaohs had, where they were buried together with all their belongings. Cigarette butts were scattered on the table and empty translucent bottles were neatly arranged at oddly regular intervals. I dropped him, already conscious, onto the sofa in front of the telly, wrapped him in blankets, and began to rub his stiffened hands with towels in attempts to bring life back into them. And the life slowly retreated back to his body from his heart, a weak old motor that was still beating and trying to push blood into frostbitten limbs but was ready to give up and halt. He was in a limbo. His fingers had taken on an ominous livid colour, and the blood would not return to them. He sat there, clenched, unaware of what was happening, unsuccessfully holding back thin, quiet moans of pain as I furiously rubbed and rubbed and rubbed his hands with the terry towel. He didn't have tea at home, so I had to pour just hot water. He sat there, dejected, wrapped in three layers of clothes, drinking, drenching himself, from my old mug, clasping it in his slightly pinkened fingers.

We sat in silence; I tried not to look at him, I didn't want to see his face and meet his eyes. I was afraid to find something I-know-not-what in his blue eyes and wondered if I should have come here at all. In a wheezing voice, he asked how I was doing. I nodded and clasped his hand in mine. Then, after an hour or two of sitting like this, I took him to the bedroom and went to sleep in my old room.

It was only as I dozed off after a series of unsuccessful attempts that I heard that fucking clackety-clack, clackety-clack, clackety-clack, the sound of typewriter keys clicking, hammering unevenly, one after another, a horde of woodpeckers against my head. Quietly, trying not to creak the floorboards hidden under the discoloured icy linoleum, I left my room and found him in the kitchen. He was sitting hunched over the table, sniffling and rasping in front of the typewriter, trying to type something with trembling, or rather shaking, hands. I watched in silence as he tried to summon the prose out of himself and press it into the paper, but his fingers wouldn't listen. He kept missing the keys, getting angry, crumpling the sheets and throwing them away until the paper ran out, and he folded his arms and lay on them and sobbed, whilst I stood by and tried to remember the last time I had cried myself.

It was two nights ago. Now, I sit here, count snowflakes, and look the fucking bullfinches right in their little black beady eyes. The papirosas have already overflowed the ashtray. I'm not sad anymore, perhaps a bit melancholic but rather... empty. All I feel is the slug creeping inside my brain and I can hear the sound of mucus coming off its ugly body. As a child, in the summer, after the storm, when the rainbow tarts itself like a bowstring in the middle of the sky, when everything scents of dust from the road, or, as I learned later, "petrichor", an earthy, fresh, sweet and woody smell of geosmin produced by bacteria in the soil, when worms and slugs and snails crawl out from under the ground and overtake all the surfaces, including stones and trees and bushes, I liked to crush them, especially slugs. My father said that I shouldn't touch them, for they carry diseases, but I didn't care. I used sticks, stones, or just boots to squash them. I always leaned down to examine the remnants, their glistening grey bodies, now flattened, ruptured and seeping that viscous mucus, crinkled like a deflated balloon that oddly chafed as I stepped on them again and again. There was something alien in them, something even demonic, ugly, unbeautiful, that I couldn't understand and accept, and still cannot. And today, despite it being freezing winter, I feel like it's raining again and I somehow feel geosmin in the air. It's in my nostrils. It tickles and itches, makes me want to sneeze, calls me to crush slugs, crush my own parasite slug, but somehow I'm too afraid that it won't die either, like the bastard, and will only grow bigger.

I bury the last papirosa in the ashtray, dress up, and, hiding my face under the hood, exit the building, leaving my still snoring father behind. People, those angry and sullen faces, pass me, looking under their feet, throwing side glances at me. I feel they are scheming something, ready to snitch on me. I'm now one step away from them putting my bloody and bruised face against the wall, getting me "disciplined", hurling my irrelevant body with thousands upon thousands of other irrelevant bodies into a pit, splattering us with diesel, and throwing a single match. The flames would explode with dark smoke and give birth to the odour of burnt skin and melting synthetic clothes. Countless particles of disintegrated corpses would fill the air, casting an ominous pallor on the city. The rays of the dying sun would strain to penetrate the haze, reduced to a faint, sickly orange glow. The cloud of ashes would unfurl its full doom, swallowing the last vestiges of light and warmth, leaving nothing but howling darkness and the rattle of death. I saw that many times, in dreams and in reality.

When the Tsar loses confidence in his guardian-snipers, with or without reason, he assigns more trusted agents to them, and before each mission, the agents give one of you snipers a blank bullet. If you attempt to assault the bastard, they immediately shoot you in the head. You don't know who gets the blanks—the agent assigned to you gives you the bullets right before the event, right after he searches you. You either kill the bastard and die a glorious death or get lead in the back of the head and die for nothing.

Dressed in white-grey camouflage, I stand spreading my hands as the agent, a man with a scarred face dressed in all black, searches me. It's always the same guy, but I don't know who he is or his name. He's a head taller than me, as wide as a cupboard, tranquil and slow in movements like a python. Without a hint of care or compassion, he checks my pupils, pulls aside my eyelids, then measures the temperature of my body, asks a set of secret questions, hands me a protocol to sign, then hands me a box with bullets. I hesitate, look into his eyes but can't read him. The thoughts are inscribed on them in an encrypted language.

Lo and behold, the square is filled with a cheering crowd that has been herded there like sheep. They wave our black and red flags with a white dove—or perhaps that bullfinch making a snow angel. They shout something; must be calling out for the Tsar, but their voices mingle with the air and the dusting snow, and the wind instantly blows them away before they reach my roof. In a minute, a chain of seven identical black armoured cars snakes down the snowy grey streets. From one of them, the bastard will soon emerge. It might all be a dream again, for I cannot remember how I got to my position. I always appear where I'm supposed to be. It's automatic, scripted, rehearsed.

Through the scope, I observe the crowd: their faces are blurred, their bodies, all monochrome, start turning into a single amalgamation. Here, the motorcade stops, and from the second car from the end appear two louts, and then the Tsar himself in a huge black fur hat, seemingly bigger than his small round head. My vision narrows and focuses on the Tsar's figure, whilst the rest gradually disappears, and again we're alone with him in an empty space, separated only by my rifle. My hands are shaking, my throat is scratchy, I want to cough. I shouldn't have smoked so much. My eyelid already seems stuck to the metal scope, and it no longer feels cold.

With barely bent knees, the Tsar walks on the paving stones, from which the ice was removed during the night. He stops to cough, and I hear how the crowd is swooning, as if expecting him to cough out his lungs in a bloody fountain and fall. Everything is quiet, nobody dashes; sheep is cordoned off by a hundred of pigs. Here he stands at the tribune and opens his mouth. I catch the aiming point right between his burly grey eyebrows.

My eyes water, my finger on the trigger trembles. Discipline, patience, stance, posture, grip, breathing— these and other of my father's words are all back in my head now. When it's all over, he'll appear out of nowhere behind my back, pat me on the shoulder, and tell me his baby girl has done well.

After I imagine it, I freeze, stop my breathing and my heart and my thoughts and my dreams, and finally take that shot.

№7: Soon

—You're allowed to cry only whilst cutting onions. I'll be back soon.

—When is "soon"?

—Sooner than you think.

Yet Myra's father still wasn't home. That careless, cherished-by-adults, and cryptic-to-the-child's-ear "soon" stretched into three hours and twenty-eight minutes, and the sound of the slammed door still haunted every glass item and each window in their cramped flat where they'd spent the past week. Myra and her mother followed all the instructions her father had given them: they found the darkest and thickest bedsheets they could in the wardrobe, covered all the windows in multiple layers, disconnected the telephone's wire from the socket, turned off the lights, lit candles, sat silently, and waited. The latter proved to be the hardest of all.

—The hand goes like this. The knife becomes part of your arm, so you can steer it safely, and it'll never swerve and cut your finger, see? Yes, and put your thumb here. Exactly. Hold tight. Now slice!—said Myra's mother, smiling.—And there you have it. Practice makes perfect.

Myra nodded nervously and, huffing and puffing, began transforming the pitiful onion into uneven, ugly slices. Her mother patted her head and moved to the other side of the kitchen.

The onion pieces that aspired to become an onion soup looked so miserable that tears welled in Myra's sore eyes. Yet she kept working with the knife ("Slice, slice, slice..."), striking it against the scuffed cutting board that reminded her of the stump on which her father chopped wood when they visited her grandparents in the village.

Little salty drops fell on the board, on the knife, on the onion pieces, which made Myra frustrated and angry. She tried to immerse herself in the process, hoping to distract herself from the tick-tocking of the enormous, eerie grandfather clock in the corner, but she still felt its presence, and the rhythm of the pendulum slicing the air in its wooden tomb matched the rhythm of her cutting onions, as if the clock itself were cutting something or someone.

—Do you know how to play hide-and-seek?

—Dad, I'm eight. Of course I know how to play hide-and-seek. But I like to play it at home,—Myra muttered.

—We can't...

—Because "dangerous people" would find us. I know that.

—See? You understand how important this is.

—Aren't they looking for you?

—They're looking for all of us.

—All of us?

—Yes.

—And me?

—And you, and your mum, yes.

—What did I do?

—You needn't worry about it.

—Now I'm worried, Papa.

—I'll be back as soon as I can.

—Where are you going?

—To check if we all can go. The news is good.

—I don't understand.

—You will, I promise.

—You promise too much. This way you'll run out of promises soon. And by soon, I mean the *real* soon.

Whether those were the same dangerous people

who'd broken into her father's performance when they were at the theatre, Myra didn't know. Who they were, nobody told her either. She overheard that they were policemen, but they didn't look like ones to her. Men in balaclavas materialised from nowhere and dragged the actors off stage. She later asked why they wore those knit helmets, and her father only joked that it was to hide their horns. She wasn't scared, unlike most of the audience, thinking it was all part of the act. Very immersive, she thought; Papa is talented. Only when her mother, who sat next to her, leaned over to cover Myra's eyes and whispered something unrecognisable did she think that maybe she didn't understand, and it wasn't a play anymore. Then her father with a few people approached them and led them both out of the circle through the emergency exit. After that "incident", as her father kept calling it, their life had turned into hide-and-seek of the highest order, and she didn't quite like it.

A brass cuckoo bird peeked from the clock's tower, and the inside bell banged. The knife slipped, scraped the board, and swept the onion pieces onto the floor. Myra dropped the knife, squeezed her eyes, afraid she had cut off all her fingers even though she felt no pain, and stood like that, frozen, listening to the clock's ringing. Ding-dong. Ding-dong. Ding—

—Let me pick that up,—Myra's mother said, approaching her.—Do you want me to finish it?

Myra gave no response. Her fingers were fine. Her mother put her hand on Myra's shoulder and leaned in.

—Go check what the radio says. I'll sort this out.

Myra sat at the table, pulled the wee wooden radio with long and thin metal whiskers selfwards, put on the headphones, and began switching channels. All she heard was ear-grating white noise. She wondered why someone would broadcast a noise like that and why not just broadcast silence instead. But every channel responded only with hissing, some with a monotonous beep, and only one of them, on which she thought the news was supposed to run, all of a sudden, with music. It featured a smooth and sultry melody overlaid with hauntingly beautiful female vocals.

—*Eternal embrace, our hearts entwined,*—the woman sang.—*In the darkness, our love shines; though death may part us for a while, we'll reunite with a tender smile.*

Myra's mother looked at her inquiringly. Myra shook her head in response and continued listening to the song.

—*And as the shadows start to fall, I hear your voice,*

The song was comforting despite its sad words. It was certainly more comforting than the news would be unless, interrupting the white noise, the reporter announced that her father was safe and sound.

If the rumours were right, the dictator was dead. She had overheard it whilst her mother and father were habitually whispering in the corridor. What "the dictator" denoted, Myra didn't definitively know. She thought it might be someone who had good diction, unlike herself, or someone who dictated something and other people had to transcribe it in orderly letters, avoiding any spelling mistakes, like in school. Maybe it was a code word for something, or maybe she just misheard it and it was "director", like her father, the one who told actors what to do because, for some reason, despite being adults, they didn't know what to do. In any case, she didn't understand why that dictator's death would make her parents excited. They weren't like that when her grandpa died, or her grandma a few years before, which she barely remembered. They were sad and even cried a little bit, even when they were not cutting onions, but she felt nothing. She didn't know what to feel because nobody told her how to act, not even her father, who, she thought, was supposed to do that by his profession yet consistently failed at it. She pretended that she was also sad but couldn't force herself to cry despite all her attempts at squinting or not blinking. "When times change and you grow up, you'll make a good actress," her father told her once, "or a director". Now, she no longer wanted to become an actress or a dictator, even if she had ever wanted to, for she didn't want to be dragged off stage one day.

Distracted from cooking, Myra's mother looked at the door. Myra put down the headphones and hushed. Someone, probably one person, was climbing up the stairs, and the footsteps grew louder and louder. It was unlikely to be her dad, Myra thought, because he would be quiet, as he had "directed" them. The room became silent except for the ticking clocks, and the "Eternal Embrace" was hissing from the headphones in Myra's hands. Her mother stepped closer to her and turned it off.

The footsteps stopped when they reached the door. Rustling of clothes. The jingle of keys against the concrete floor. A double knock. Myra's mother approached the entrance, looked through the spyhole, and breathed out. She opened both latches and the chain, and then the door.

There, panting, stood Myra's father in a snow-dusted overcoat. He was smiling and held a large white cardboard box in both hands. He bent down to pick up his keys and stumbled into the flat.

Myra jumped from her chair and ran to hug her father.

—Dead,—he declared.—The Tsar's dead.

He ruffled Myra's hair and handed her the box. She carried it to the table, opened it, and an alluring aroma wafted into her nostrils. It was a cake, a three-layered honey cake with a creamy filling hinting at orange zest, adorned with intricate golden leaf patterns radiating from the centre to the edges like sunbeams.

With the black bedsheets still over the windows, they spent the evening together, eating cake and drinking tea. Myra's parents laughed and behaved as if the world outside the flat didn't exist anymore. But Myra couldn't help but feel a pang of confusion, wondering how soon she would learn how to feel happy about someone's death.

I hereby cast beams of appreciation to...

My dear wife Katya
for her love, support, encouragement,
and valuable feedback

David T., Jeanne T.,
Konstantin A., and Oleg V.
for reading this book early
and providing editorial support

Sam McF.
for typing the intro letter

Felix K.
for extra proofreading and fixing commas

Everyone E.
who helped to make this book real

Russian F.
for inspiration

and you, Dear R.
for reading

Explore more of Vanya Bagaev's work at

Nova-Nevedoma.com

including literary, experimental, and speculative fiction.

Expect weird characters in whimsical situations, a lot of unhinged dialogue, absurd and dark humour, dreamlike sequences, helical narratives, hysterical surrealism, magical realism, sudden philosophical and psychological romps, stylised prose, often infused with poetry, witty comedy, poignant twists, Russianness, logic and lunacy, and many other matters of interest.